FAMILY HOLIDAY

The summer for Clare, Guy and the children brought the holiday — like every other year. It also brought the chance meeting with Blake Randall, the young officer she'd loved years ago in a wartime hospital. And whereas Guy was the kindly but unexciting doctor she had married, Blake and Clare felt the same spark of their youth. Soon they were unashamedly head over heels in love again, but when the holiday ended, she would be separated from Blake forever . . .

DENISE ROBINS

FAMILY HOLIDAY

Complete and Unabridged

LINFORD
Leicester

First published in Great Britain in 1937

First Linford Edition
published 2013

British Library CIP Data

Robins, Denise, *1897 – 1985.*
  Family holiday.- -(Linford romance library)
  1. Love stories.
  2. Large type books.
  I. Title II. Series
  823.9'12–dc23

  ISBN 978–1–4448–1399–9

Published by
F. A. Thorpe (Publishing)
Anstey, Leicestershire

Set by Words & Graphics Ltd.
Anstey, Leicestershire
Printed and bound in Great Britain by
T. J. International Ltd., Padstow, Cornwall

This book is printed on acid-free paper

for The Family

For, Day, my holiday, if thou ill-usest
Me, who am only Pippa, old year's
  sorrow,
Cast off last night, will come again
  to-morrow
Whereas, if thou prove gentle, I shall
  borrow
Sufficient strength of thee for new
  year's sorrow.

ROBERT BROWNING

Clare believed devoutly in the joys of family life.

She had determined from the time her children were born that they should know those joys, because she had never known them. 'My own children shall know what it is to have a proper background — a nice house and good parents.' And she had tried to carry out her word.

But now she was uneasily aware that the 'children' were fast becoming young men and women . . . and that they were beginning to pull in opposite directions . . . For some reason Clare could not quite put a finger on, this frightened her.

BOOK ONE

1

It was during breakfast on a wet, grey morning in April, which had more of the chill of winter than the warmth of spring about it, that Mrs. Tardy broached the subject of the family holiday.

'It's time we fixed up something,' she said. 'You know what it was like last year. If you don't book rooms in time, you get bad ones.'

She made her little speech brightly, with the cheerfulness of one who is not certain that her suggestions will be well received. But there remained the necessity to show an optimism whenever she, herself, felt the reverse. Upon that optimism, Clare Tardy had built the foundation of the family happiness. One severe crack in it and the whole edifice might fall to the ground. In other words, she considered it of vital importance that she should hold the family together. For although nobody said anything, she had a faint but growing belief that they had begun to pull in opposite directions.

There was, of course, a tendency for members of modern families to lead their own lives. Clare Tardy was not blind to that fact, neither was she old-fashioned, nor anxious to impede progress. She was too intelligent. But she did dislike disintegrated families, just as she hated hotels, except for short holidays, or a flat — which in her estimation lacked the atmosphere of a real home. She liked a house and a family in the house. She believed devoutly in the joys of family life.

She had determined from the time her children were born that they should know those joys, because she had never known them. Her own mother had died when she was a child. Her father, who was in the Indian Army, remained abroad, and most of her childhood was spent at school or staying with elderly aunts.

When she was of age, the Great War came, and her father was killed on active service. Once again Clare had to face an existence without any permanent background. Being of an affectionate and sociable disposition, she had loathed it.

'My own children shall know what it is to have a proper background — a nice big house and good parents,' she had said from the day that she married. And she had tried to carry out her word.

But things never seemed to work out according to plan. And Clare's marriage had by no means been exactly what she had hoped for.

Here, at the breakfast-table, sat the family; puppets, just as she might have placed them on a stage in her imagination. But unfortunately she could not perpetually pull the strings. These puppets were much too human.

Guy, her husband, was a doctor with a small but steady practice; Jack, her eldest son, was twenty and up at Oxford. They had gone to many sacrifices to send him up, but there he was, thank God, studying Law and doing quite well. Joan, aged eighteen, had just left her finishing school in Lausanne. And Margaret, affectionately known as 'Mogs', aged fourteen, was still at a boarding-school in Hastings.

Here they all sat, in the big, solid dining-room of a big, solid house in South Kensington, outside which was a brass plate with the inscription: *Dr. G. B. Tardy, M.D.*

The house was much too big for them, of course, and they could not afford as large a staff as was necessary to run it efficiently. But they always seemed crowded in the holidays, and when the children brought friends to stay with them. It was easier, of course, when Jack was at the 'Varsity and Mogs at school, and there were only three of them left.

Guy had done quite well. He was popular amongst his patients. But with his family he was almost shamefully negative. He never bothered about any of them. Clare felt that he never bothered much about her, either. To him, they must all be like pieces of furniture in the house, which he had grown accustomed to seeing and which had their proper uses. But none of them seemed to have any bearing upon his particular private life. He worked, ate, slept and played his Sunday golf. They saw little of him except at the morning and evening meals.

More often than not he came into his food after they had all finished. Such were the exigencies of his calling. He was frequently out in the evenings, too. And when at home, he either went to sleep or listened to one of his immense collection of Bach records.

Bach was Guy Tardy's religion. Clare was fond of light music but had never shared in his passion for the classics. Those endless Masses and Fugues appeared to her noble and beautiful, but she could see no reason why anybody should wish to sit down and listen to them for hours, and feel those hours to be the high spots of living.

She regretted, somewhat, Guy's tendency to be old-fashioned and insular in his views. He hated speed. He had a car only because it was necessary to his work. A solid British car which he never drove over thirty-five miles an hour, even on the open road.

He was always kind, affectionate, and ready with nice presents at Christmas and on birthdays, but otherwise entirely vague.

Clare had, for a number of years, been virtually head of the household, the one to whom the family went when they wanted something bought, or something done. She liked that. It gave her a feeling of warmth and ownership. Without being over-possessive, she expected some attention and gratitude from her children, and while they were at school she had received both. In fact, it was while they were very young, despite the fact that Guy had then only a small practice in Earls Court, and they sometimes had a frantic struggle to keep up appearances, that Clare had known real happiness.

Very soon after her marriage she had ceased to demand much from Guy as a husband. She had been a pretty girl with an ardent and impulsive nature. She had always woven romances around doctors and been proud and pleased to marry Guy Tardy who, in the third year of the war, when they married, was a medical officer attached to a Red Cross Unit in Camberley.

He had never been handsome, but fresh, auburn-headed and quite attractive in his uniform. His vague, rather dreamy manner had drawn Clare to him. She was his antithesis. So much more spirited. And at that time, his devotion to music had been part of his attraction for her. She liked to think she was marrying a man with an artistic sense. Their honeymoon had been a fair success. Afterwards, Clare devoted herself to forwarding his medical career.

At the end of the war, he bought a practice in Earls Court. All too soon there had come an end to the romance which Clare's nature craved. With the birth of Jack, the immersion of Guy in his work and her endless duties as wife and mother, the lover in Clare was soon put to sleep. That had been Guy's fault more than hers. He had never had a strong sensual side and he was much too busy and too tired during the first years of marriage to delve into psychological problems about his wife.

If at first Clare had resented the loss of that more exciting quality in marriage which a normal woman craves, she had soon settled down to the lack of it and concentrated on the family.

But now the family were growing up. They were becoming independent. It frightened her. She was no longer the one to whom they looked solely and absolutely for their physical and mental needs.

Almost daily she was feeling the little tugs — Jack and Joan and even Mogs, still a schoolgirl, pulling away, away from her. Thinking for themselves, acting for themselves.

It was not that Clare was exacting. She had always deplored the type of women who wound themselves round their children, sucking their youth like vampires, forcing gratitude or respect from them — or at least demanding the outward semblance of what could never really be extracted by force. But she did love her three children devotedly and she felt a kind of desperate urgency to keep them with her a little longer. For once they were gone she would have only Guy. Guy, who was just a figure-head, wanting to be well-fed and looked after but requiring none of the spiritual intensity of affection which she had it within her to lavish.

She had had so many little blows of late. Jack, for instance, when he last came down from Oxford for vacation, spent most of his time away with the friend who had shared rooms with him. And she had so looked forward to his coming home. She adored her son. He was handsome and gay. At the same time, he had inherited some of his father's quiet persistence in work, which was of enormous value. He was to go into the office of his uncle, Arthur Tardy, who was a solicitor in the City.

More than anything in the world, Clare liked to have Jack with her, and he was devoted to her. While he was still at school he had been proud of her because she had kept her youthful figure, dressed well and could still be called a very pretty woman. It was always 'Mum' who got him out of his little scrapes. She had helped him only last term when he had exceeded his allowance and run into debt at Oxford. Yes . . . they had always been close friends.

Yet these last twelve months Jack had not appeared to need her quite so much. Unpacking his trunk for him at Easter, she had come across the photograph of an unknown girl, which had fallen out of one of his pockets. That had terrified her. To think that

Jack had a mysterious girlfriend and had said nothing to her.

She was too tactful to question Jack, but she had entertained a dozen fears since that moment. Who was the girl? Perhaps she wasn't very nice. Perhaps Jack didn't care to introduce her to the family. It would be so awful if her attractive, handsome boy got himself involved with some undesirable female. And it was grievous to Clare Tardy to feel that she had been left out of his confidence. It made her wonder, too, if there were a lot of other things she did not know.

Then there was Joan. A beautiful girl, Joan. Looking at her seated at the breakfast-table, Mrs. Tardy felt proud of the fact that she had produced such a daughter. Joan had her mother's dark eyes and slim, graceful build, and Guy's reddish-brown head. Tawny, naturally wavy hair, always beautifully done.

She was a reserved girl, with a stubborn side to her nature. Guy had that same stubbornness. It was best left alone. When Joan was reprimanded, she shut up like a clam.

While still at school, Clare had not found it so hard to cope with Joan. There was a sweet, pliable side to her and she loved her mother. There was, then, the artificial stimulus of excitement over school holidays, that joy of being home again which Margaret was still experiencing. But after Christmas, when Joan left Lausanne, made away with all her ugly school clothes, started to have her hair 'set', to put colour on her lips, to 'grow up', in fact, Clare had felt uncomfortable about her. The girl seemed so aloof. She had never been as communicative as Jack or Mogs, and Clare found it hard to discover where she went or what she was doing. When questioned, sometimes Joan would give a full account of her activities, but usually she was non-committal and even annoyed by the most innocent questions, as though she resented any inquiries into her private and personal life.

Clare, who had herself always been a

frank, impulsive person, failed dismally to understand that side of Joan.

There remained Mogs, the humorist of the family. Overgrown and in the fat 'puppy stage', with curly hair which was a frank and flaming red, and sincere blue eyes. Not really pretty, but full of vitality and charm. Clare had never had trouble with Mogs and had congratulated herself that she never would have any — until last term when Mogs developed a 'crush' as she herself termed it, for her music-mistress at St. Brede's.

That 'crush' had a psychological effect upon the fourteen-year-old girl which was devastating and had appalled her mother. All through these holidays, Mogs had been different. She had lost her sense of humour.

How Clare loathed the name of Miss Walters! How willingly she could have administered a dose of Guy's prussic acid to that woman. For consciously or unconsciously, she had taken Mogs away from her. The Christmas holidays had been so different. Jack and Joan might have other things to do, other people to go out with, but Mogs was usually the devoted daughter who had to include 'Mum' in everything. Now Clare missed that devotion and was ridiculously jealous of Miss Walters and the influence which she appeared to have over the child.

If Clare maintained that there was to be no revolution in Central Europe, Mogs immediately said:

'Oh, but Mum, Miss Walters says there *is* going to be one.'

When Clare said:

'I don't like the way you are doing your hair, darling. I wish you'd brush it back from your forehead,' the answer came:

'But Miss Walters *likes* it done this way!'

And so on, until Clare wanted to scream.

It was not as though Miss Walters, estimable teacher of music though she might be, had anything in particular to recommend her. Clare had once talked to her at St. Brede's about her girl's musical tastes and had thought the woman rather second-rate. But she seemed to exercise a peculiar magnetism over Mogs who said she was 'simply too marvellous' and that a lot of the other girls 'simply adored her'.

It was a schoolgirl-stage, through which Clare had once passed. Looking back, she could remember at her Convent, a nun of peculiarly unattractive mien who had inspired her to exaggerated admiration. It was a form of hysteria to which schoolgirls are given, generation after generation. And with girls of Mogs' age, it was, of course, a kind of sublimated sex. Unhealthy in a way, yet natural. In another year or two, all that emotionalism would be directed towards some young man.

Somehow, Clare felt that she would not mind when her beloved Mogs worshipped a young man. But she did most strenuously dislike the adoration and exaltation of Miss Walters.

However, with the tact and good sense which were inherent in her, Clare made no outward fuss or objection. She even allowed Mogs to talk unceasingly of her adored one.

But it did annoy her when she found her own photograph, which always hung over Mogs' bed, replaced by a most unattractive, out-of-focus snapshot of the music mistress (taken at St. Brede's with Mogs' own Brownie and framed at Woolworth's). Clare's own likeness had been relegated to the dressing-table. But Miss Walters must be guardian of the bed! Really, it was laughable! But Clare was jealous and admitted it to herself.

2

This morning, when Clare broached the subject of the family holiday, she did so with a trepidation which she had never before experienced. She was not at all sure that the holiday would be as big a success as those of former years. But she was determined that they should, as usual, go away together. That holiday was the thing Clare most looked forward to in the year. Those three weeks when, with Guy and the three children, she abandoned the cares of housekeeping and they had fun together somewhere by the sea.

In Clare's mind were stored away countless precious memories of holidays, right from the time the children were babies, until now. She liked it when they all took a look at the fat albums full of snapshots, which they liked to laugh at, now. To Clare, those snapshots, often badly taken, had their amusing side, but they were sacred, too. Pictures of her loved ones in all stages.

Brightly and hopefully, this morning, Clare talked about the forthcoming summer, looking round the table with that wide smile which had always been her chief charm:

'It may be early to talk about it, but we must make plans and book the rooms. Don't you agree, Guy?' she said.

Dr. Tardy dropped his newspaper and rose to his feet. He was a slight man of medium height. He wore the striped trousers and black coat which he considered appropriate to his calling. He did not approve of the young physicians who went their rounds wearing ordinary lounge-suits or 'tweeds'. He was a stickler for 'good form'. He took off the horn-rims which he used for reading.

'Well, my dear, I suppose so. I haven't actually given a thought to our holiday.'

That was typical of him, thought

Clare. For when did Guy ever make plans or lay schemes apart from his work? He always left things to her. Sometimes she wondered what would happen to him and the children if she died. Guy was a dutiful parent, saving and making what provision he could for the future, denying himself — and her! — in order to save for a rainy day. But he was not the sort of man who worried about the lesser problems or attended much to the lighter side of life. She had never known him come in and say:

'*Let's do this or that . . .*'

It was she who made the suggestions and he fell in with them affably enough, so long as nothing interfered with his job.

Watching him this morning, she thought, not for the first time, that he had begun to look much older just lately. He was only five years her senior, but she looked much younger than Guy. There were very few grey threads in the smooth darkness of her hair. (She had cut it short, and been 'permed' to please Joan.) But Guy's auburn locks had thinned and vanished until he was almost bald on the top of his head. The fresh complexion which he had had as a young man had become an unattractive brickish-red. He still wore the small military moustache which he had grown in the war, when he had become a captain in the R.A.M.C.

His eyes were very blue. Margaret had those same eyes, and there was something very appealing in them. They were so honest. They had that gentle, dreamy quality which unfailingly strikes the maternal chord in a woman's heart. But although Clare could be furiously angry with Guy, and had been so a great many times during their married life, angry and bitter at his lack of perception except for his own particular needs and his apathetic attitude towards everything other than work and music, she could not say that he had been anything but a good husband.

Today, however, in her forty-second

year, she wondered how she had ever managed to feel the slightest thrill in his embrace.

She turned to her elder daughter.

'Don't you agree, Joan, that we ought to start thinking about the holiday? Otherwise we'll find all the best places booked up.'

Joan looked up from the grapefruit which she was eating. It worried Clare because the girl had lately started to 'slim' so drastically. She had nothing now for her early morning meal but grapefruit and coffee. It didn't seem enough, and her father had told her that from a medical point of view she was being a little fool. And it was all so absurd, since she was quite slim. But she maintained that she had to 'keep down the fat'.

She said:

'Well, as we never go to the best places, I don't see that it matters.'

'Darling!' said Clare reproachfully. 'That's not very nice of you.'

Jack, tackling two eggs and some

bacon, cast a sinister look at his sister.

'She isn't really very nice, Mum. There's a lot behind that Mona-Lisa face of hers, if you ask me.'

'Well, she isn't asking you,' said Joan. 'And anyhow, you don't know anything about me.'

'I do!' put in Mogs. 'I saw you shove a letter under your pillow this morning when I came into your room, and I bet it was a secret.'

'Don't sneak, you little rat,' said Jack, and administered a swift kick under the table which made Mogs draw in her ankle with a scream.

Dr. Tardy clicked his tongue.

'Tch! Tch! Really, really!'

Clare shook her head in silent reproach to all. She took no real notice of such talk. She knew that the children were all really devoted to each other. Mogs was, perhaps, a little resentful of the older sister, who was inclined to be what she called 'bossy' and superior. And Jack was her great favourite. But they all got along together very well.

24

Nevertheless, Clare wondered a little why Joan should flush such a flaming red and look quite so furiously at Mogs. Had she received a letter which she didn't want any of them to see?

Mogs, afraid that she had said something that she really ought not to have said, made things worse by announcing that she 'did not suppose the letter meant anything' and 'that she hadn't meant to sneak'.

'Oh, be quiet,' said Joan and turned to her mother. 'Must we have the usual gathering of the clans at the seaside?'

'Surely you like our holidays, darling?' said Clare.

Joan finished her grapefruit.

'Oh, yes.'

'It was all right last year up at Cromer,' said Jack, getting up and feeling in his pocket for the pipe which he had just begun to smoke. 'Old George and I had grand sport fishing.'

'Well, I shall get away at the end of July as usual,' said Guy Tardy. 'Now I must be off. Goodbye, all of you.'

He walked to his wife's chair, put down a cheek which she kissed, and with the paper under his arm, left the dining-room. Outside they could hear his familiar cough. Guy always had a throaty cough first thing in the morning. Too much smoking, he said.

Joan poured herself out some more coffee and gave a deep sigh.

'What's that for, dear?' asked Clare.

Joan looked at her mother in an exasperated way.

'Can't one even sigh in this house without being cross-questioned?'

'That's what I say,' put in Mogs, deciding that she had better back Joan up about something in order to get into her good graces again.

Clare, hurt and uncomprehending of this attitude, cast a look in her son's direction. He gave her no help. He had hardly been listening to his sisters. He had drawn aside the net curtains and was staring out at the street.

'Blasted awful day!' he muttered. 'Never does anything but rain in this infernal country. I wish to God I could go to a place where there was some sunshine.'

'Then you're not patriotic,' said Mogs, with that triumphant tone of one who has found a justifiable reason for offering criticism to her elders.

Jack ignored this. Turning back from the window, he said:

'I shan't be in today, Mum. Chris rang up last night and asked me if I'd drive up to Oxford with him and get some books he left in my digs, so I said I would.'

Joan Tardy also rose from the table. She put her hands in the pockets of the blue wool cardigan which she was wearing, and drew it tightly around her, accentuating the slender lines of her young body.

'I can't think why you bother to come down for vacation, Jack. You're always going back,' she said. 'This is the third time you've driven up to Oxford since you came home.'

Jack, pipe between his teeth, gave her a frozen smile and bowed from the waist.

'Exactly! And can't one take a drive to Oxford without being cross-questioned?' he mimicked her.

Clare Tardy shook her head. She wiped her lips on her table-napkin, leaving a faint daub of scarlet on it. Inadvertently, she deplored the fact that lipstick made such a mess of the table-linen and she wished there need not be this bickering. It had only recently become so frequent in the family.

'Darlings!' she said. 'Do be a little more friendly. What *is* the matter?'

Jack walked to her side and put an arm around her shoulders.

'Don't look so tragic, love! We don't mean it. It's the weather. We'd all be better for a spot of sun.'

'Miss Walters says we're in for a wet summer,' announced Mogs.

'I'm sure Miss Walters is a very fine prophet,' said Clare. 'But let's hope she's wrong.'

'She's right about most things,' said Mogs, with a fervour which relapsed into gloom. 'I thought there'd be a letter from her this morning,' she added.

'You only heard from her two days ago,' Clare reminded her.

'She writes such marvellous letters,' said Mogs.

'Oh, well, darling. You may hear tomorrow,' said Clare, swallowing her secret loathing. 'And now, while we are all here together, do let's try to settle the question of the holiday. You know Daddy doesn't mind where it is so long as it's by the sea and comfortable.'

'Which I can't say it ever is,' said Jack, removing his arm from his mother's shoulders and going back to the window.

She followed him with loving gaze. Her precious Jack! Six-foot-one of good looks, with her own dark hair and eyes. He had a brown, clear skin and rather a wide, curved mouth. Certainly much more like her than his father. And like his grandfather on her side, who had been such a handsome man. Clare was not quite sure that she liked the way Jack dressed at the moment. She did not care much for those brightly colored pullovers and the suède shoes. But all the young men of today seemed to affect this careless way of dressing, and what did it matter so long as Jack was healthy and happy?

'I know the beds aren't like the ones in our own home, but one doesn't expect that when one goes away,' she said.

'It would be all right if we could go to one of the big hotels,' said Joan. 'But we can never afford it.'

'The biggest aren't always the best,' Clare tried to console her.

'Dear Mum!' said Joan, shaking-her head. 'You and your clichés.'

Clare had never really grown accustomed to the adverse criticism which she got from the family, but she rarely made open protest, unless one of them was definitely rude. And that she would not stand, for she considered it bad for their characters to allow them to become impertinent.

'Well, dear,' she said, 'if we can't afford the big hotels it's no use worrying. We must just put up with the other kind, or take a cottage.'

'Don't let's do that,' said Joan quickly. 'It would mean a lot of beastly cooking and washing-up.'

'But it was such fun down in Cornwall.'

'When we were kids,' said Joan scornfully.

Clare looked at her elder daughter with a humorous lift of the eyebrows.

'Well, since you're so grown up this year, darling, why not make some intelligent suggestion about the holiday.'

'I don't particularly want to go anywhere.'

Clare took no notice of that. She presumed that Joaney was in one of her bad moods.

'What do you suggest, Jack?'

'I don't see why I shouldn't be consulted,' said Mogs in an aggrieved tone.

'By all means, darling.'

'Then let's go to Eastbourne.'

'Good God, why?' said Jack.

Clare maintained a frozen silence. She knew why. Miss Walters lived there. She said nothing more about Mogs' suggestion, but again put her question to her son. He showed no particular enthusiasm.

'Oh, Devon or Cornwall, I should think. You fix something, Mum. You usually do.'

Clare looked at her three children with some uneasiness.

'I'd so much rather go where you all wanted to go.'

It was on the tip of Joan Tardy's tongue to say:

'Except for Mogs, we none of us want to have the holiday.'

But she saw the futility of saying any such thing. It would only hurt and upset her mother, and if she, Joan, asked to be allowed to stay here in London, which she most devoutly wished to do for private reasons of her own, the request would be refused. So why make it? Even Jack, who was the eldest and could, on the whole, do as he liked, wouldn't be allowed to remain here. The house was always shut up for the three weeks of their father's holiday, and the servants all sent away.

'No suggestions?' said Clare anxiously.

'Eastbourne — ' began Mogs.

'Run upstairs, darling, and tidy your bedroom.'

'Well, where *are* we going?'

'We'll fix something this evening, dear.'

Mogs departed. Jack followed her, announcing that he must keep his appointment with Christopher. Left alone with her mother, Joan said:

'I've been asked out to dinner tonight.'

'That's nice for you, dear,' said Clare. 'Who by?'

'You don't know them,' said Joan.

'Mayn't I even ask the name?' Clare could not resist the tiny inclination to be sarcastic.

'It's some people I met at the Metfords' cocktail party the other night. A brother and sister. Her name's Agatha Downe. She and her brother, Anthony, are frightfully clever dress-designers.'

'Oh?' said Clare vaguely.

She had never heard of the Downes, but she knew the Metfords and liked them.

Then Joan added in a slightly nervous voice:

'Do you think I could have my next month's allowance in advance?'

Clare, lighting a cigarette, glanced at her elder daughter through the haze of smoke and frowned faintly.

'You know Daddy and I don't approve of that, Joan. It's a bad principle — like borrowing. After all, you get six pounds a month, which is as much as we can manage, what with Jack being up at Oxford and Mogs' heavy school bills, and — '

'Oh, I know all that,' broke in Joan impatiently. 'You're awfully good to me, Mummy, but it is hard to manage when one's got to be dressed decently. I make a lot of my own things, but sometimes one must have a decently cut evening dress. You see, I've been asked to a party with the Downes on Monday night, and they're all so frightfully chic. My blue's too ghastly now and the white's worn out.'

'Are the Downes so wealthy and well-dressed that you should appear shabby beside them?'

'Don't be silly, Mummy. I've told you they're important dress-designers.'

'You mean they have a shop?'

'Yes, in Berkeley Square.'

'Well, wouldn't they make you something cheap?'

Joan Tardy flushed as brightly as she had done when Mogs mentioned the letter.

'You can't expect me to ask friends

that I've only just made to put their prices down for me,' she said in a haughty voice.

When she used that tone she could always manage to make Clare feel quite stupidly inferior to her eighteen-year-old daughter. It annoyed her. She said:

'Then you'd better wear the blue net or get the white ironed. I don't think you should attempt to live above your station. It's silly to try.'

Joan lost her colour. Clare recognized that as a sign that she would soon lose her temper. The girl had plenty of control but she seemed to suffer from a kind of inner torment of feeling. Clare would have given anything to be allowed to help her, to be admitted into her confidence, to feel that she really knew and understood her. And why be so upset about this question of the allowance? It was not really like Joan. She usually managed very cleverly on her six pounds a month. Bother these Downes and their chic clothes!

'Then you won't advance me the

money, Mummy?'

'I'd rather not — ' began Clare.

'You want me to be thought shabby?'

'Darling! I've never seen you look shabby. You're always very well-dressed. Everybody says so.'

'Your friends may think so, but mine have a different idea of dressing.'

'Darling, have my friends such very different ideas from your own? I'm always nicely dressed, aren't I? You've never said that I've got bad taste.'

'Oh, it's nothing to do with that, Mummy. I know you always look nice. But you don't exactly move in the same sort of set as I do.'

Clare remained silent a moment. She caught a glimpse of herself in the mirror which hung over the sideboard. There she stood, in a grey suit with a dark-brown jumper. Red on her lips, her nails coral-tinted, a cigarette in her hand. It didn't look like an old-fashioned figure to her. But of course she was another generation from this girl and had to remember it. If she were modern — Joan wished to be ultra-modern. Joan had those dark brows of hers plucked, and used black on her lashes. That reddish, lovely hair of hers was cut short and done in a fashionable coronet of curls about her brow. Joan felt it deeply when economy forced her to wear anything that was 'no longer being worn'. She had come back like that from her Swiss school. Heaven alone knows, thought Clare, why parents sweat and stint themselves to send their children to finishing schools, which seem to turn healthy, simple schoolgirls into discontented, exotic young women of the world!

She did not object to Joan being exotic so long as it was not carried to extremes. But she did wish she would not always talk and behave as though her mother were prehistoric.

'Well, Joaney!' at length Clare said with a sigh. 'I may not understand exactly what you need, but I think I do, and I must say I find no fault with what you wear and I shall think nothing of your new friends if they criticize you.'

'They may not criticize me, but I shall hate what I've got on, that's all!' Joan flung at her mother, and turned and walked out of the room.

It was not a serious enough altercation to make Clare think about it for long. She had other things to do. She must go downstairs and see Cook about the food. Then there was the laundry to be put away.

They had an Austrian girl in the house at the moment as a house-parlourmaid. A beautiful needle-woman, and a great help with the mending of the house linen and family clothes. But her English was not very good and Clare had to do the laundry-lists. It was really wonderful the way this big London house was run by two and a daily woman. She was lucky to have Lucy still. Lucy had been their cook for twenty years. She was of the old school and not anxious to make continual changes. Of course, she had her drawbacks. There were a great many complaints from the children about lack of variety in the dishes served up to them. What Lucy did was good, but she had her limitations. However, Clare felt lucky to have her. An old retainer. There were few left.

Thinking about the staff reminded her that their 'daily', Mrs. Benson, was 'walking out on them' next week. A 'char' must be found to replace her. That was a nuisance, because Mrs. Benson had once been in good service and answered all the 'phone calls for Gerda. It wouldn't be easy to replace her. Clare reminded herself to go along to a Registry Office this afternoon.

There was Mogs' return to school to be thought about, too. That trunk to be gone through. A long list of 'wants' for the summer term loomed in front of her. Mogs had grown so plump that she would soon burst everything that she had been wearing last summer term.

What was it Jack had asked her to do, when he said goodnight last night? Ah, yes! To have his white waistcoat cleaned. He was going to some party.

She mustn't forget that. Those were some of the little things Joaney might have helped her with but never did. She was too busy thinking about her own affairs.

'I wonder what would happen to them all,' pondered Clare Tardy this morning, 'if I suddenly changed and began to think of nobody but *myself?*'

BOOK TWO

1

Clare Tardy went down to the kitchen to order the meals for the day.

What a nuisance it was that one had to bother about food. To eat is a necessity, but why should one have to trouble oneself to think up dishes that everybody in the family would like, day after day? Guy was easy enough to cater for. It was the children who were difficult. Joan, with her slimming. Jack, who wouldn't eat anything greasy, insisted upon things being served up as though they were in a restaurant, and prided himself upon being a gourmet. And dear old Mogs, who copied whichever one of the family was her favourite for the day.

Half-way down the staircase, Clare met Gerda. A big, jolly, healthy girl with her flaxen plaits and china-blue eyes. She always looked nice. Wore pretty red or blue dresses which she had brought from Austria and delightful embroidered aprons. When they had a dinner-party she would put on a real Tyrolian costume, which was enchanting.

But Lucy disapproved of 'foreign nonsense', as she called it. There she stood, by the kitchen sink, in a faded pink cotton uniform with the stiff white embroidered collar of thirty years ago. She had a very proper cap on top of her neat grey head. She was a little, dried-up woman, with a long, disapproving nose, and gold-rimmed glasses through which she regarded the goings-on of a modern world with supreme disdain. A faithful chapel-goer, was Lucy. A conscientious worker — one who would be described in a reference as 'clean, honest and respectable'. Bitter about those who got on the wrong side of her. Loyal and devoted to those whom she liked. And Dr. and Mrs. Tardy came under the latter category. She had come to them when they were a young married couple.

It had never entered her head to leave them, except for one giddy lapse, just before her fortieth birthday, when she had 'walked-out' with the milkman. For a few intoxicating weeks, Lucy had contemplated the awful intimacies of married life. After all, she had her bottom drawer and her Post-Office savings, and it was the right and proper thing that a girl should marry, and wrong to live in service for the rest of her life.

Unfortunately, however, the milkman, of more ardent disposition than Lucy, so far forgot himself one evening as to make to Lucy what she afterwards described in anger and shame as a 'horrid suggestion'. A suggestion which was replied to in no uncertain manner by a blow from Lucy's umbrella and a stream of virtuous scorn — which would, surely, have enhanced her already blameless reputation amongst the congregation at her chapel, could they but have heard it.

The net result was that the contents

of Lucy's bottom drawer remained untouched, like Lucy's impeccable person. And here she was, aged fifty-nine — at least so she said, although Clare was convinced Lucy had seen sixty long ago — unmarried and likely to remain so. Of her private life Clare knew little, except that she had a mother still living in a Derbyshire village. This mother Lucy visited on her annual summer holiday and from her she received regular presents at Christmas and on her birthdays. Little china ornaments, discreet knitted garments, crocheted mats, and nearly always a framed text. Lucy's collection of texts adorned her bedroom at the top of the house.

The family, who had on occasions peeped into that bedroom, adored Lucy's texts. For years they had shone from the walls on her side of the room, devoutly scorning the frivolous possessions of the numerous young house-parlourmaids who passed through the house and through Lucy's hand.

Grimly, Lucy looked upon the younger generation. Her Spartan and censorious attitude was really a drawback, because young maids wouldn't stay with her. Gerda was a success, however. Fortunately, she understood only half of the criticisms and godly advice which poured from Lucy's lips over a cup of tea or at night, after she had risen from her prayers and prepared herself for her virtuous slumber.

Gerda was good-natured and laughed at everything. There were times when Clare envied the girl that innate buoyancy, that inclination to throw a dazzling smile upon the world, no matter what happened.

Lucy greeted her mistress with the usual: 'Good morning, M'm,' which came from her thin, puckered lips tartly enough, although she showed less acidity towards Clare than to any other member of the household, and was really fond of her. She was fond of them all, at heart.

Lucy rolled down her sleeves, wiped

a chair for Clare, bade her be seated and stood before her at attention, like a soldier receiving his orders.

'Mr. Jack will be out to lunch, Lucy. The rest of us will be in,' said Clare. 'What can you suggest?'

That question was automatic. But Clare never received anything more helpful from Lucy than:

'A nice piece of steak,' or:

'A nice piece of fish.'

So long as it was 'nice', Lucy bothered little about the manner of serving it.

This morning, she said:

'What about a nice piece of meat?'

Clare sighed. Her dark, bright eyes roamed round the gloomy kitchen which Lucy kept spotlessly clean, and she thought how sadly it needed a coat of paint. Her mind would keep wandering to the holiday and her secret worries connected with it. She could not put her mind to food. She said:

'It had better be a joint, I suppose.'

'A leg of Canterbury would be nice,' said Lucy.

Clare frowned. Would it? As far as she herself was concerned, she cared little what she ate, although she thoroughly enjoyed a good meal when she was taken to a restaurant or was out at a party. It was always such a joy to eat something one hadn't ordered oneself. Jack didn't like lamb very much, but he was out today, so perhaps the 'Canterbury' would do.

Clare had meant, when she entered the kitchen this morning, to arrange something a little new and tempting. She departed crestfallen, having given way to insidious hints from Lucy that a 'Nice rhubarb tart and a custard' would be 'ever so nice after the joint'.

So unoriginal! But she really hadn't time to sit down and look through the cookery-book. She wondered some-times if all those thousands of recipes were ever tried out by anybody, or whether the average mother of a household fell back on the monotonous diet of joints, chops, fried fish, and the unchanging list of sweets.

Part nights were especially a menace to Clare. For them, Lucy had but one unfailing menu to suggest:

'A nice chicken and a nice trifle.' (The latter, with its dash of sherry, Lucy would never touch, herself being strictly teetotal!)

'Oh, dear,' thought Clare, as she climbed the stairs again and went towards her bedroom, 'I *do* look forward to my holiday, this year.

She felt suddenly tired. She would hardly dare admit, even to herself, that it was the family and her countless unexciting little jobs which tired her so. If she were slack and dispirited, she put it down to the lack of sun and the fact that her inside had been a little troublesome lately. She was apt to get a nagging little pain across the back. Something not quite right since Mogs was born. Guy said a small operation would cure it, but she had never consented to have one. It was neither serious nor essential and she couldn't be bothered with operations. But when she got specially tired, the pain was worse.

The aching back had come to be an accepted fact by the family and was known as 'Mummy's Pain'. News of it was received with annoyance rather than with sympathy. To the children, it had generally meant little more than a deterrent to their particular desires.

The Pain was there this morning, dragging at her as she walked up to the third floor. She put a hand on her back and rubbed it. There was a lot to be done. Mrs. Benson did not arrive for an hour, and before that Clare liked to get the rooms tidy so that Gerda and Mrs. Benson could get on with the cleaning straight away.

The telephone rang. There was an instrument in Clare's bedroom, and there she answered the ring.

All day long there were calls for the doctor, and messages to be taken down.

But this call was for Joan. A man's voice — unknown to Clare.

'May I speak to Miss Tardy?'

'Who is it, please?'

'Who is that — ' came the answer, rather rudely.

Clare stiffened.

'It's Mrs. Tardy speaking.'

Before the man could answer, there was a click. Then came Joan's voice. She had answered the call down in her father's consulting-room.

'It's all right. It's for me, Mummy.'

'Oh, very well,' said Clare.

She put down the receiver conscientiously, although she would like to have listened-in. Who was the young man? He had quite a nice voice, but no manners.

A few moments later, she heard that it was the great Mr. Downe, himself. The dress-designer of whom Joan had been telling her that morning.

Joan burst into her room, flushed and breathless, and with none of the ill-temper shown at the breakfast-table.

'Mum — isn't it marvellous? Anthony Downe has asked me to get to their flat early, because we are going on to a First

Night. It's the new revue — 'Keep Sing-ing'. I've never been to a First Night. And then we're going to have supper afterwards at some club, and dance.'

Clare smiled. She loved Joan like this — when the superior young lady became a natural, excited little girl.

'It sounds lovely, dear.'

'I've always wanted to go to a First Night. It *will* be a thrill.'

'You'll wear your white, won't you?'

The vivid look in Joan's eyes died down. The mention of the dress brought back the unpleasant argument in the dining-room. But she was too excited about her invitation from Anthony Downe to keep up any ill-humour.

'I expect so,' she said. 'I must get Gerda to help me iron it.'

'Now don't take Gerda away from the bed-making,' said Clare anxiously.

But Joan was out of the room, calling:

'Gerda! Gerda! *Wo bist du?*'

She liked to use on the Austrian girl

little bits of German which she had learned at Lausanne.

Clare shook her head. That meant that Gerda would have none of the beds made before Mrs. Benson came. How thoughtless the young were! They and their wants must always come first.

'I suppose I was the same when I was young,' thought Clare.

But she could not remember being quite so selfish or egotistical as Joan. She thought, with a glimmer of humour, that that was possibly what every past generation said about the present.

She felt rather mean, not letting Joan have her next month's allowance in advance. The girl was so set on having a new party dress. But she mustn't weaken. It would be bad for Joan's character.

She didn't much like the sound of this Anthony Downe. Most ill-mannered, that peremptory demand as to who *she* was.

Clare walked into the bathroom, so

big and spacious that it served as Guy's dressing-room as well. There was an air of Spartan severity about Guy's compactum wardrobe and that solid mahogany chest of drawers, on top of which sat his brushes, a bottle of brilliantine, nail-scissors and file, a collar-box and two leather-framed photographs. One, of the three children taken together at a later date than the little one which Clare treasured. The other, in fading colour, of herself, which was still in the case in which she had given it to Guy before their marriage.

A very young, rather wistful Clare, her dark hair puffed out in a chignon, in the style of 1915, cheeks delicately pink, red lips smiling. Nothing much but her face, her long, slender neck and the rest of her fading away in a cloud of nebulous chiffon. Typical of the 'pretty-pretty' coloured portraiture of that time.

Many a such photograph had rested against many a heart under a khaki tunic during the Great War. Today, twenty-three years later, photography was different. That last one taken of Joan, a clever enough study, showed Joan's profile reflected in a mirror and seemed to Clare rather hard and striving for effect. But that's what they did, nowadays, these young people. They claimed to worship at the shrine of simplicity, and their very simplicities were affected.

Clare looked at that wistful young girl on Guy's chest of drawers and thought:

'That was really me. I was so romantic. So trusting and full of hope. That's what I shall always be. They'll never make a hardened cynic out of me. I enjoy smoking. I like an occasional drink. I want to fly. I quite like lipstick, nail-varnish, hair-sets and new clothes. But I *do* like the softness and the sweetness of the old days. They call it being sloppy — they play swing music instead of ballads about moonlight and roses. They count wise-cracking and a kind of insolent bravado higher than old-world courtesy or charm. They want independence before they're really fit to depend upon themselves. They like noise and speed and give themselves no time to think. If they *have* to sit down and think, they're bored. Well, I'm not like that — not really. And I never shall be.'

Recently, she had wished that she could talk to her husband more intimately about the children and these changing times. It would be nice to have someone who understood and who would be helpful and sympathetic. For there were moments, and they were becoming more frequent nowadays, when she felt very much alone — defencelessly so — in the midst of her growing family.

She picked up a grey silk tie, folded it and put it in one of the drawers. While she did so, it struck her that the greyness of that tie was symbolic of Guy and his existence. It could truly be called colourless.

People and their lives were really rather like colours. The violent, turbulent people were the flaming reds and yellows. The half-and-halves were the blues and greens. The quiet, the sorrowful, the negative people were the browns and mauves and greys. She could think of everybody she knew in terms of colour. And some were queer mixtures, half-tones, stripes, indeterminate. She fancied that she, herself, was rather like that. Indeterminate. Yet there was a streak of flaunting colour somewhere deep down inside her. Only it had been subdued for so long that she had, on the surface, become as monochromatic as Guy.

She didn't like that feeling. She would like to call back some of those gay, flaunting colours of her youth. Had Guy ever had any? She began to wonder. No, there had never been anything turbulent about Guy. Even their courtship had been quite mild on his side. She had really been the passionate and emotional one of the two.

She wondered, as she put away Guy's tie, what it must be like to be married to a man who might be symbolized by more brilliant hues. An impetuous, gay kind of man. One, for instance, about whom she could not say:

'I know everything that he is thinking and everything he is going to do.'

The sort of man whose desk might be locked. She was not a prying woman, but she knew that she might look through any of Guy's possessions and find nothing to excite or interest her. Nothing to make her jealous.

But why, at forty-two, bother to wonder what marriage to another man would be like? Shameless! And so early in the morning, too!

2

Clare went from Guy's dressing-room up to the next landing. She met her younger daughter coming out of her room. Mog's plump young figure was attired in a ready-made tweed suit which fitted nowhere. With it she wore a jumper of a startling orange which she had knitted for herself and which clashed violently with her hair.

With some amusement Clare looked at her. Sometimes she wished that she had enough money to dress her two girls extravagantly and exquisitely. But one would have to be very rich indeed to keep up with the development of Mogs' curves and remain chic!

'Where are you off to, darling?'

'To get some stamps.'

Mogs was clasping a letter to her bosom. Obviously she had written to Miss Walters.

'Then I want to go to Woolworth's,' added Mogs.

Clare nodded. She never inquired what Mogs wanted at Woolworth's. Her expeditions there were numerous and secret. Often small presents were purchased and given as peace-offerings to one or another of the household whom Mogs thought she had offended. She had a touchingly generous disposition.

'Your gloves, darling,' said Clare absently.

'Oh, must I — ' Mogs began.

'Don't be silly, darling. You know you can't go out without gloves.'

Grumbling, Mogs returned to her bedroom and fetched the most despised and hated articles of her wardrobe.

After she had gone, Clare marvelled at the persistence and obstinacy of the very young. Day after day and week after week, Margaret Tardy sought to slip from her house gloveless, and remain so.

Clare passed into Mogs' bedroom to

see that all was in order before Mrs. Benson started cleaning. All was certainly not in order. No amount of stern discipline, cajoling or of reproaching could make a tidy girl of Mogs.

The bed had been made. That was one job which Clare insisted upon both Joan and Mogs performing in the house before they did anything else. Mogs' face-towel was on the floor. Her sponge had been left on the eiderdown, from whence Clare hastily removed it, shaking her head when she saw the large wet stain. Shoes were flung in various directions. An open drawer in the dressing-table showed such wanton confusion that Clare hastily shut it. It wouldn't bear looking into twice.

Her roving gaze was caught and held by the photograph of the cherished Miss Walters over the bed. Above it was a large portrait of Ivor Novello, whom Mogs had worshipped since she was thirteen. Unframed, and jammed into the wall with four drawing-pins was Mr. Novello.

The walls were, for the most part, concealed by favourite pictures. Cheap seaside photographs of fat, uninspiring little girls — Mogs' friends. Hockey groups. Long, narrow framed verses about dogs, cats or birds. A large colour-print of an Alsatian's head. Mogs adored anything to do with dogs, and Alsatians in particular. She asked regularly every Christmas if she could have her own dog, knowing that she would always be refused, poor darling. They could not have dogs in a London house.

The top of Mogs' dressing-table was a revelation. It was quite a small piece of furniture, but on it were crammed as many small objects as could be placed there. All the family likenesses. Daddy in his R.A.M.C. uniform, bearing at that age a strong resemblance to Mogs herself. A head and shoulders of Clare in evening dress. An excellent enlarged snapshot of Joan on a horse. The breeches and polo jersey suited Joan admirably. Jack, imposing in cap and gown, at Oxford.

Then a galaxy of brushes, combs, manicure-set; a cheap, blue glass powder bowl — Lucy's gift on Mogs' last birthday — which Mogs had filled with the cheapest powder. It gave forth a formidable perfume. A pottery vase, modelled by Mogs at school. Out of it drooped a bunch of faded silk poppies, bought on the Armistice Days of several years past. A small magnifying mirror, one of Mogs' greatest treasures. When she had nothing else to do, she examined her face for spots. She had reached the age when they were frequent. She was painfully self-conscious about them and was not to be discouraged by frequent warnings from her mother that she should 'leave them alone or she would get blood-poisoning'.

With some amusement and much love in her heart, Clare looked around this room, so typical of her young daughter. Whilst deploring the lack of order, Clare missed Mogs sadly when the litter was put away and the door shut, which meant that Miss Margaret Tardy was back at school.

Jack's room, now. At the very top of the house, with a half-sloping ceiling, and a window which had quite a pleasant view of chimney-tops. Just a bare, masculine room, almost as disorderly as Mogs'.

A pair of shorts and a sweater on the floor. (Every morning Jack put them on and went up a ladder through a trap-door in the roof and did exercises. His daily rite.) A pile of dirty linen in a corner. Blue pyjamas, spot-silk dressing-gown, two shirts, waistcoats and trousers hanging over the end of the bed, waiting to be disentangled.

Little on the walls in this room, except one enormous etching of Jack's college at Oxford and a rough sketch of a woman's nude body, headless, and with enormous thighs and ankles. Clare thought this superlatively ugly, but Jack assured her that it was a work of art, done by some young man up at Oxford whom everybody hailed as a second

Epstein. Jack had reached a stage where he thought he knew something about art. Possibly due to his friendship with Christopher Fenlick, who was studying painting. And as none of the other Tardys knew anything about it at all, nobody disputed Jack's authority on the subject, nor dared deny that the headless torso and legs of the gargantuan female were drawn by a master hand.

Clare folded Jack's clothes. Made a bundle of his washing ready for the laundry basket. Removed a pipe and a box of matches from under the pillow. Shook her head at the sight of a burn on the sheet. Reminded herself that they were running short of linen, and that she must replenish the cupboard at the next goods sale. Then withdrew from the room.

A year ago she might have done some tidying in the drawers. Not today. Jack was no image of Guy, whose life was so open. Clare had never recovered from the shock of finding that unknown girl's photograph in Jack's trunk. She was terrified of what else she might discover. She did not want to come by chance upon his secrets. She wanted to be told. And if she were not told, she preferred to know nothing.

She walked down the stairs, looking at her wrist-watch. It was nearly ten o'clock. Plenty to be done before lunch. This afternoon she must settle down to letter-writing.

Since the family had left it to her to arrange the holiday, she fancied she knew a place which they might try this year. Kymer Cove, in North Cornwall. She had seen it advertised in a Sunday paper. The Headland Hotel, right on the sea. Good surf-bathing, riding, tennis and 'reasonable rates', according to the advertisement. She would send for the brochure and ask the manager for terms for a family of five. Kymer Cove was not very far from Newquay. Clare knew Newquay quite well. She used to stay there as a child.

Her next thought was:

'I want a cheque out of Guy for the housekeeping.'

One of the things he generally remembered was to give her a cheque on the first of the month. This time it had slipped his memory.

She went down to the consulting-room. Dr. Tardy was there, putting some instruments into his case. He glanced over his shoulder at his wife and gave his vague, impersonal smile.

'I'm just off, dear.'

'Have you time to give me my cheque before you go?'

'Your cheque . . . Tch! . . . Of course, I meant to write it out last night.'

He put down his case and seated himself at the roll-top desk. A good, old-fashioned desk which had belonged to his father, a general practitioner in Lincoln, where Guy had been born and lived during his boyhood.

This was one of the rooms in the Tardy house which nobody criticized or attempted to change. It was Guy's own territory, not to be invaded or altered with the progress of time. It was arranged exactly as had been the other consulting-room in their house in Earls Court. Desk at right-angles to the window, which was curtained with brown velveteen. Leather arm-chair for patients, who must sit with their faces turned to the light and the critical gaze of the physician. Red Turkey carpet. Big walnut cupboard with glass case, behind which were unimposing rows of Guy's shabby medical books. In the cupboard, all the instruments neatly arranged in rows. Guy never allowed anybody to touch them. He dusted that cupboard himself. There was a wash-basin behind the screen in the corner. A couch with a brown blanket folded at the foot, used for examining patients. A gas-fire set in an old-fashioned grate, over which was a mantelpiece of carved oak with a bevelled mirror set in it. Nothing very modern here except the electrically-run gramophone upon which Guy played his records.

Clare had sometimes let herself go so far as to visualize the up-to-date consulting-room of a young physician. One could combine beauty with utility these days. It could be a wonderful, exciting room. But she never did more than think about it. She never even suggested to Guy that he should modernize his sanctum. He would have dismissed the idea as being unnecessary and much too expensive.

She stood there, watching him write the cheque for her. Somehow, the sight of him bent over his blotter, using that rather scratchy pen, made her feel a motherly tenderness. It might have been Jack, as a schoolboy, at his homework! Guy was a simple child in so many ways. Yet so incredibly old — so set in his habits. Walking through life in a rut which he had no intention of leaving.

If she had ever dreamed of Guy becoming a great and flourishing doctor, one of these distinguished men who are consultants at the big hospitals, or who sit in splendour in their Harley Street houses, raking in big fees, she had long since abandoned the dream. Guy was not meant to be one of the great. He was just typical of thousands of others in his profession, who go along steadily and without distinction. Well, they were, after all, as necessary as the great stars in the firmament. And Guy had his following. He inspired confidence in many. Every Christmas, Clare had to cope with presents, not often desirable, from his 'grateful patients'.

He held the written cheque out to Clare, shut his desk and locked it.

'There!'

'Thanks, dear.'

She smiled at him and he smiled back. They were good friends after a fashion. Yet all real contact between them was absent. On the occasions — rare these days — when Guy was physically stirred by his wife and she submitted to his familiar and uninspiring embrace, they still lacked that real contact which she had always wanted, but which he, so temperamentally different, seemed not to miss.

She had an unusual impulse this morning to draw near to him. As a rule she was too busy with the family and her duties to be introspective, but she was still deep down in her a creature of impulse. There were times when those impulses broke through the armour of indifference under which she hid her psychological yearnings. An armour which she supposed must be worn by a million wives who had been disappointed in marriage, but who would never dream of voicing the fact, either to their husbands or anybody else. Wives to whom marriage was an institution to be accepted and upheld like religion or politics. Necessary institutions to the civilized, full of flaws and drawbacks, often disillusioning and depressing, yet necessary. And those who doubted too much, rejecting sacrifice and good faith, were the deserters and the renegades.

Oh, that armour was of vital importance! And in it, women fought for the peace and security and happiness of family life, which is, after all, a thing of national importance. Only of secondary value were the thrills and joys of complete personal fulfilment. Clare Tardy had reached a pitch when she had little time or inclination to dwell on the thought of, or even admit the need for, personal ecstasies.

But here she was this morning, conscious of a strange restlessness for which she could not account except that it was the spring, and that she felt herself to be of less importance than usual to the family, therefore of more importance to herself.

She said:

'Guy, couldn't we do something a little unusual for our holiday this year?'

He regarded her doubtfully over the rim of his glasses.

'Unusual? What do you mean?'

'Oh, I don't know — go abroad,' she said recklessly. 'I think the children are a little sick of England.'

'Sick of England!' repeated Guy Tardy, as though he had just heard a great heresy declared in his presence.

'Well, my dear, I mean we've always spent our holidays at home. Why shouldn't we go to France or Germany this year? You'd get some lovely music in Germany,' she added with guile.

He shook his head.

'I think it would be out of the question, taking the children abroad. Much too expensive.'

'If we could afford it, would you like it?'

He snapped the clasp of his bag together.

'I don't think so, dear. I don't think there's anything like England for a holiday.'

She abandoned her madness. She was too philosophic to pursue an ambition once she was discouraged. But she felt suddenly cross and said:

'I wish you'd do something out of the ordinary, *sometimes*, Guy.'

He stared at her. It was the rarest thing for Clare to be cross or critical, or to attempt to divert him from his ordinary course. It was a course which he pursued without deliberate unkindness or egotism. It would never enter his mind that he might be either cruel or selfish to lead his life just as he wanted it and abide by old traditions and habits as his father had done, and his father's father. He behaved in what he considered a normal and just fashion. He hoped and believed that he conducted himself as his wife and family expected of him. And he was a man incapable of sitting down and asking himself how far he fell short of those expectations. He had his private worries. His little arguments and upsets with Clare. His parental responsibilities. But they were what every husband and father had and, in his estimation, were not vital problems. Everything seemed to be going along quite well and nobody appeared to him ill or unhappy. So why worry?

He had vague recollections that Clare as a girl had been temperamental, and there were, of course, times when he did not quite understand her. There had been times, too, when he had found her a little too exuberant for him, mentally and physically.

But it was years since he had given any thought to that problem. He fancied the babies and her busy life looking after them, and running the home had quietened Clare down. He admired her, trusted her and was devoted to her, just as he was devoted to his son and his two daughters. He would die, if necessary, for any one of them. But much less easily could he have changed any of his little habits and customs for their sakes.

He supposed that today Clare was put out about something, which accounted for what she had just said. For why should he do anything out of the ordinary?

'What's the matter, my dear?' he inquired.

78

'Oh, nothing,' she said abruptly.

'That's all right.'

'No — there is something — really,' she corrected herself. 'The children are getting more and more independent and soon they'll be going their own ways and getting married and we shall become grandparents, and then — '

'Well, what then, my dear?'

'Do you *want* to grow old, Guy?'

'My dear, I never think about it.'

'Well, I do. And I think we should both make an effort to keep young.'

'What, pay visits to Dr. Voronoff?' asked Guy, with his heavy humour.

She frowned and shook her head.

'I'm not talking about our bodies.'

Guy Tardy cleared his throat. It was such a long time since he had had a discussion of this kind with Clare that it almost embarrassed him. Now, why on earth must she take it into her head to talk about such things this morning when he was just off on his rounds? And anyhow, what did it matter if the children did get married soon and have children of their own? It was the natural order of things for him and Clare to become grandparents. Perhaps women felt this growing old business more than men. They were such queer, illogical creatures. Discontented as a sex. Much more discontented than men.

He patted Clare's shoulder.

'You don't look like growing old, my dear. You'll make a nice young-looking grandmother.'

'Oh, well — it doesn't matter!' she said gloomily.

'What doesn't matter, dear?'

'What I really feel.'

He moved towards the door. Clare knew that he was anxious to avoid talking to her. He had always been like that. He was a lot better at examining bodies than minds. Dear old Guy! Her crossness evaporated and she even felt sorry for her little outburst. But she could not resist throwing a sudden wicked little shaft after him.

'Do you know, Guy, your friend Dr. Cordman told me at dinner the other night that I looked like Joan's sister, instead of her mother. I've been losing weight lately. Don't you think I *am* looking rather nice?'

He turned at the door and smiled in his vague, kindly fashion. Was she any thinner? He hadn't noticed it. Perhaps she was. Certainly she was very slim for her age. Remarkable, too, how she had kept her pink and white complexion and the blackness of her hair. He didn't like that stuff she put on her lips these days. Still, he supposed it was the smart thing for women to do. He had no suitable response to that mischievous look in her eyes, but he attempted to endorse what his colleague had said.

'Certainly, certainly, you might be Joan's sister, my dear.'

She thought:

'Poor old dear, it's a shame to tease him.'

But she went on:

'Then you be careful that I don't get what Joan calls a 'boyfriend'.'

That sent Guy Tardy altogether out

of his depth. It was much too frivolous. He made no attempt to answer the challenge. He waved a hand at her.

'I must be off now, dear. Bye-bye!'

The door shut behind him.

Clare, left alone, stood for a moment looking at the pink slip from Guy's cheque-book, held between her fingers. The impish look had died from her eyes, and with it much of the youth and vitality from her whole face. She thought:

'It would never enter Guy's head to imagine that I am capable of looking twice at any other man. And I don't suppose I am.'

She went out to do her shopping, feeling rather ashamed of herself, but still not cured of her restlessness.

BOOK THREE

1

Two good-looking young men wearing grey flannels, brown suède shoes and exuberant ties, drove along the main London road in an open M.G. with a roaring exhaust. They were heading for Oxford. Both were hatless. The driver had long fair hair which blew about in the wind. He was of fair complexion, with delicate features and a wide, sensitive mouth. One slender hand held the wheel with nonchalant grace. Christopher Fenlick looked what he was — an artist — with an air of effeminacy which was counteracted as soon as he spoke by his deep, agreeable and thoroughly masculine voice.

His companion, of broader build, dark and tanned, a complete physical contrast in every way, was Jack Tardy. Side by side in the car, the young men might have been of the same height, but actually Jack was almost a head taller than Christopher.

Their friendship had begun two years ago, when they had first met, living in the same College. Later they had shared rooms in an old, winding street leading off the High. Despite the fact that they were following such different professions, they had many tastes in common. Books and pictures in particular. They got along admirably together. It was a definite blow to Jack when, two terms ago, Christopher went down before him in order to study painting at the Slade School. But they continued to meet in London. And such expeditions as these, going back to the University town, were a delight to them both.

How many times, thought Jack this morning, had they rushed up this same road in this same car, racing against time to get back into College after a night in town. Only once had they come to grief in that car, and that was during Christopher's last term and second year, when they had both got 'tight', landed themselves in a ditch and been 'gated'.

Great times, and Christopher had admitted that once he went down, life hadn't seemed as grand or gay, and would never be so again in quite the same way. He envied Jack being still up. But Jack was not altogether enjoying himself these days.

Without Christopher's constant companionship, he had become a little bored, and boredom had led him to seek feminine society, which he had never done while Christopher was with him, apart from the girls who came up for 'Commem' balls, or a little harmless dalliance with a local barmaid.

Jack had found rather more than he had intended when he went seeking. An 'affair', in fact, of a magnitude which was causing him a great many sleepless nights and considerable heart-burning.

In Christopher Fenlick alone had Jack confided his affair with Amanda Deering. Amanda was on his mind, and it was a relief when he could get away from the family and talk about things. Chris had been pretty sympathetic and helpful, one way and another. But in spite of all Jack's efforts to get the truth out of him, he was never quite sure whether or not Chris approved. Perhaps it was that he didn't wish to dampen the enthusiasm of anyone so obviously in love. But Christopher was definitely guarded in his opinions and his advice concerning Amanda.

Of course, Christopher knew Amanda, as did most of the men up at Oxford. For the last couple of years she and her sister, Sheila, had been running a school of dancing and had made a popular thing of it.

Nobody knew much else about the sisters, except that they lived on the Woodstock Road in a little house with their father, who was reputed to have been at the 'Varsity in his time. Certain rumours had recently been circulated that old Deering had been at one of the colleges, but in the capacity of a scout rather than an undergraduate. Jack knew as little as anybody of Deering's origin and cared less. It was enough for him that both Amanda and Sheila seemed nice, well-brought-up girls, and that any man would be proud to go out with either one of them.

On one occasion, Jack and Chris had taken both the sisters for an evening's amusement and Jack had fancied that Chris might become interested in Sheila. But he had not done so. His interest in the majority of pretty girls, he maintained, was aesthetic rather than physical. He liked to draw impressions of Sheila's head and figure. But any real admiration or emotional stirring which Christopher might have had for Sheila had been killed stone dead on the day when he had suggested, dispassionately, that she might sit for him in the nude. This had brought forth from her an indignant protest of: 'Oh, you are *awful*!' Since then, he had labelled her a provincial little fool and had never asked her out again. He and Jack had had an argument about that. Jack, upon hearing the reason for his friend's disdain, made a feeble effort to defend Sheila.

'After all, old boy, if she is a nice girl and that sort of thing, she might not want to take off all her clothes.'

Christopher had patted his arm and said:

'Very delicate, old boy. Very understanding. Almost as 'refeened' as the lady herself.'

That had provoked the one and only quarrel they had ever had. And it had ended in Christopher's admitting wearily that perhaps Sheila had misunderstood his intentions, but that it seemed a great pity that artists were the only men who could appreciate a woman's figure from the aesthetic point of view. Added to which, he felt that an intelligent woman would have turned down his suggestion quietly and firmly if she didn't want to sit in the nude, and need not have put the most vulgar construction upon it.

The quarrel had left no rancour. But the subject of Sheila was never referred to. What Jack felt about Amanda was different. He was at a stage, himself, far too boyishly crude and physical, to appreciate the painter's ability to gaze on the uncovered female form with purely intellectual appreciation.

However, Christopher was very sporting about Amanda, and Jack was eternally grateful to him for these occasional lifts to Oxford.

'I wish to hell,' said Jack today, 'that I could get out of this summer holiday my mother's planning.'

'Where are you going?'

'Don't know yet. Devon or Cornwall, probably. Mother always fixes something. I think these family gatherings are pretty grim.'

'I'd rather like one, myself,' said Christopher.

'That, my dear old thing, is because you are an orphan of the storm and haven't got a family to get on your nerves.'

'That's possibly true. If I had any people, I dare say I'd quarrel like mad with them.'

His parents had died in his early boyhood, both in an airship disaster. Christopher had spent most of his life at school, and his holidays with an uncle and guardian. Fortunately for him, the uncle was a rich man and an art-collector, who offered no protest when Christopher chose art as a career. Since leaving Oxford, Christopher had occupied a small studio in Chelsea, where he was very much alone. He thought Jack a lucky fellow to have that nice family. He was an immense admirer of Clare Tardy. Joan he still thought of as the schoolgirl she had been when he first met her, although recently, when he had seen her at their house in town, he had become aware that she was growing up. He had told Jack that he admired her colouring and would like to paint her. But so far, he had never been able to pin Joan down for a sitting.

She always seemed too occupied.

'Of course you know what I'd like to do,' went on Jack.

'What?'

'Go abroad somewhere with Amanda.'

'H'm?' said Christopher.

'Oh, I know it's impossible,' said Jack gloomily. 'But that's what I'd like and so would she.'

'I bet she would.'

'You don't think my affair with her will ever come to anything, do you, Chris?'

Christopher stepped on the brake sharply and brought the car to a standstill with a violent jolt.

'Blast these people who don't let you know they're stopping.'

He drew out the M.G. They roared round the ancient saloon which had paused, and continued their course. The woman at the wheel of the saloon looked after the racing car and said to her husband:

'Nasty, noisy little brute! These boys in sports cars are a menace on the roads.'

Jack remained gloomy and preoccupied for the rest of the journey. He was really worried about Amanda. He had wondered a great many times lately why poets raved about love. It caused a lot of trouble and wasn't an unmixed blessing. He was so hellishly restless and unhappy apart from Amanda, and not too happy with her. All right when they were in each other's arms, but when they weren't, there always seemed to be a lot of arguing. It could have all been much easier had she been a girl whom the family knew and liked, and whom he could have taken home and said proudly:

'I'm going to marry her.'

But how could he take Amanda home? She wasn't at all the type his parents would like or understand. Even Joan might be a bit superior about it. His age was the main trouble. Thank God, he'd be twenty-one next year. Then no one could dictate to him.

His depression only lifted when he saw the familiar spires of Oxford rising proudly into the grey mists of the April morning. He loved Oxford. It began to rain as they drove over Magdalen Bridge. He had so wanted to take Amanda out somewhere where they could talk. Of course, it wasn't term and the town was fairly deserted, but it was all so difficult in cafés or cinemas. Perhaps they could go back to her room, where she gave her dancing lessons. Providing there were no lessons going on this afternoon.

They drew up at 'The George'. Amanda was to meet Jack there for lunch. Christopher was going on to spend an hour or two with the fencing-master who was a friend of his.

Jack climbed out of the car.

'Meet you here again at half-past five. That'll give us time to get back to town for dinner.'

'Okay,' said Christopher.

He looked at his friend standing there, careless of the rain which beat down on his black head. The artist in Christopher was stirred, as it had been stirred a hundred times, by the magnificence of Jack Tardy's vigorous youth, his perfect health, his brown, handsome face.

One of the nicest chaps he had ever known, Jack. It was a darned shame that little tart, Amanda, had got hold of him. That was all she was and he could think of something worse to apply to her, too. The rotten thing about it was that he couldn't say what he thought, or attempt to warn or discourage Jack. With Jack in his present state of infatuation, interference would soon end their friendship.

Christopher had seen through Amanda from the first, just as he had been quick to discover the cheapness and vulgarity of soul underneath Sheila's outward dignity. He only hoped the old boy wouldn't do anything crazy like marrying her. It would be an awful thing for Dr. and Mrs. Tardy.

He felt rather guilty for aiding and abetting the affair by bringing Jack up here. He had felt that, the last time he looked into the clear, trustful eyes of Jack's mother. Still, with no opposition in his way, and if he saw plenty of Amanda, Jack might soon get tired of her. Or, perhaps, Amanda would eventually give herself away.

Christopher caught sight of a girl in a grey flannel suit, with a bright green scarf tucked in the neck, waving through the glass doors of the entrance to 'The George'. Amanda, herself.

Christopher put his foot on the accelerator. He didn't want to meet Amanda. And he knew she wouldn't want to meet him. She was well aware that he had no use for her, and that, given half a chance, he would attempt to break her friendship with Jack. Ten thousand pities that Jack should be such a babe about women. Christopher, only two years older, felt quite elderly beside Jack when it came to the subject of sex. He did not feel that in his most vulnerable moments he would have been taken in by Amanda. Perhaps that was because of the years he had spent abroad, at Monte Carlo and Biarritz, with his uncle, who changed his mistresses almost as often as he changed the art treasures in his gallery.

Christopher had been flung into the company of women of all types at a much younger age than Jack. This affair of Jack's had decided Christopher that there was far less chance of the young men on the Continent being seduced into marriage with impossible women, than the average English boy, who is segregated from women from his preparatory school days onward; who is physically repressed all through his adolescence and later represses himself because of the standards with which he has been brought up. Little wonder that a healthy, vital creature like Jack should find himself on the rocks at the first call of the first really clever siren.

So thought Christopher, as he drove away from Jack. But there were none of these forebodings in Jack's mind as he leapt up the stairs and greeted his heart's desire. The mere sight of Amanda was sufficient to banish the misgivings of the journey.

He caught both her hands in a grip which made her wince.

'Darling!'

Amanda Deering smiled from beneath her lashes, pouted and rubbed her fingers.

'Ooh! You're so strong.'

'Sweet, did I hurt you?'

'I liked it,' she murmured.

He took her arm and they found a table. He ordered her the White Lady which was her favourite cocktail, and a lager for himself.

His ravished gaze travelled over her from head to foot. He liked that well-cut suit and the jade scarf. She was hatless. Amanda never wore a hat.

'You look grand! And it's heaven to see you again, Mandy.'

She sat back and dived into her bag for powder-puff, comb and mirror.

'Heaven to see you, Jackie-boy.'

If anyone at home had called him 'Jackie-boy' he would have protested violently. But from the lips of Amanda it sounded all right. Anything that Amanda said was fine, so long as it was in his favour.

'How's Sheila?'

'I left her giving a lesson.'

'Have you been working all morning, my poor little sweet?'

'Yes,' she said, with her baby pout which enchanted him. 'Much too hard.'

Under the table his hand found her knee and pressed it.

'God! If you knew how much I wished I could take you away from it.'

'I wish you could. Oxford's frightful when you're not here.'

'I like to hear you say that.'

She could have added that Oxford was always frightful out of term, when there were few young men to amuse her, but she wisely refrained. She sipped her cocktail and began to tell him about some man who was in love with Sheila. Jack hardly heard her. His whole being was concentrated upon Amanda.

In his opinion, Sheila Deering didn't begin to be as attractive as Amanda. Christopher said that Sheila was more perfect from the classic point of view. She was tall, fair and stately. Amanda was small, of the elfin type, with indeterminate features and a mass of fair hair which she wore after the fashion of many film stars, combed smoothly down to her neck, then bunching out in glistening curls. She used a lot of make-up, had long, black, sticky lashes and a big mouth rouged to a pillar-box red, which Jack found very exciting. She looked eighteen, gave her age as twenty-four and was actually thirty-one. But that was not obvious until the make-up came off, and neither Jack nor anybody else had seen her other than as a very finished product.

Jack had thought himself pretty lucky when Amanda singled him out from the other men friends she had made and admitted that she had 'fallen for' him. By the time he had dragged that admission from her, when he had run her out to Godstow for a drink at 'The Trout', last term, he had already fallen for her in a big way. He had been a little bored by dancing until he had started to dance with Amanda. Now it seemed part of life — just as she was. Nothing more thrilling than the sensuous rhythm and movement with Amanda in his arms. And a first-rate dancer she had made of him. She had said that she was 'pleased with her pupil'.

'Not so pleased as the pupil is of his mistress,' Jack had answered in a hot, unguarded moment which had resulted in Amanda growing white, except for the rouge on her high cheekbones, giving him a long, significant look from her tawny eyes — like a panther's, he described them — and saying:

'*Am* I your mistress? I didn't know.'

That had put ideas into Jack Tardy's young and impetuous head. They may already have been there, but he would never have dared express them had it not been for that slip of the tongue, and its immediate response from his dancing-instructress. He had never seriously held a woman in his arms, but he was soon to know the thrill of it. From that night onward, Amanda lived with him on the understanding that as soon as he went down from Oxford and started his career in his uncle's office, he would marry her.

He wanted to marry her. He was deliriously in love, with that consuming kind of love which a very young man feels for an experienced woman older than himself. And Amanda was certainly experienced. She could not altogether play the 'innocent little girl, seduced by the big, bad boy', with Jack. Only up to a point could she protest any kind of innocence.

It was Jack who went to her arms with white and unsullied page of youth. She took care not to admit the many blots on her own, but she had to own up to a 'disastrous marriage' made, she told Jack, when she was nineteen. Jack readily believed the story of that marriage. He burned with indignation on her behalf when she sobbed out the tale of the Naval officer, one James Mackie, ten years older than herself, who had beguiled her into believing he was a decent sort, had married her and made her life a hell. Finally — desperate to get away from him and his cruelties — she had consented to be divorced. She could prove nothing against him, and because of his reputation in the Navy, he had refused to let the divorce be on her side.

So much had to be told Jack, since he was to marry her and must see how she would be described on the licence.

She had dropped the name of 'Mrs. Mackie' and gone back to 'Miss Deering'. It was better for work, she said, and she wished to blot out the 'horrible memory' of those years spent with the Naval Commander. There was no tale of brutality that Jack had not heard of the said James Mackie. Many a time, holding Amanda's trembling little body in his arms, Jack had looked over her curly head and sworn that one day he would rout out that monster of iniquity and avenge this poor child.

And Amanda saw no reason why Jack should ever discover that James had been a very quiet, dull man, whom she had caught by spinning her 'little-girl' web across his eyes when she was teaching dancing down in Portsmouth ten years ago. Nor that she had been found by James in the bedroom of a brother-officer, two years ago. (A more hardened cynic than James Mackie, who had found it convenient to rejoin his ship at once, since he had no intention of taking on the burden of Amanda.) Nor that there was a child of that marriage, a boy, who had bored her when he was a baby and whom she had been glad to leave with his father after the divorce.

She had made no attempt since then to see her husband or her son. She had put them into the limbo of forgotten things. As she gave her age as twenty-four, it would hardly do for her to admit the existence of a son who must now be nine.

Jack Tardy's good looks, his vitality and charm, had captured her from the moment he had entered her dance academy. The chief 'snag' in her eyes was his lack of means. She had made a mess of her first marriage, and her second she wanted to be a success. She was thirty-one and could not long keep up this atmosphere of golden youth. It was time she had a husband and a settled home, if only to serve as a background.

She was always trying to persuade Jack to break the news of their affair to his people. But he said it would be a mistake. His mother might be sympathetic, but his father would pooh-pooh the idea of his marrying before he came of age. As for Uncle Arthur, who was to be his boss — a very practical, hard-headed business man — he would possibly shut the doors of the office on Jack, which would do no good. Jack was being trained for the Law and it would be madness to waste all those years of training and attempt anything else.

Amanda agreed with that. Amanda was willing to wait. But not too long.

The longer she waited, the more chance there would be of Jack discovering something about her past. Not only the marriage and the child, but one or two other episodes which had taken place since and which would not stand the light of discovery.

But Jack's main trouble was how to see enough of Amanda at the moment, and to give her a proper place in his life, without upsetting the family or jeopardizing his future.

2

'How did you manage to get up here for the day?' Amanda asked Jack, when she was drinking her second cocktail. Amanda liked her *apéritifs*, and it would never enter her head to ask herself whether a boy of twenty on an allowance could afford to buy her so many drinks.

'Oh, it was simple,' he said. 'One thing I will say about the family is that they don't interfere with what I do.'

'In the small ways,' said Amanda significantly.

Jack pushed back a strand of dark hair which had a habit of falling across one eye. It was a slightly nervous gesture.

'I suppose it's only natural that they should concern themselves with the main issues.'

'M'm,' said Amanda, and put down

her glass. Her lips had left a bright smear of rouge on the rim. She felt a secret grievance against this family of Jack's.

Jack's hand was caressing her knee again.

'Angel — you aren't getting sick of me, are you?'

One of her hands, a greedy little hand with pointed fingers, varnished to a bright red which matched her lips, fluttered daintily on top of his.

'Silly! You know I'm not.'

'I'm so frightfully in love with you, Mandy. But I tell you that so often you must be tired of hearing it,' he said.

She was a little moved by the fervour and sincerity of him. And there was something about the clean, handsome youth of his which never failed to give her a 'kick'. No, she wasn't tired of Jack *that* way. But she was a bit sick of the present situation.

Passionate encounters with Jack in her dance-room long after it was supposed to be shut up and locked for the night; stolen days on the river; a few hours in a borrowed car. That was all young and breathless and exciting in its way. But the greater part of the delirium was enjoyed by Jack. Amanda had been a married woman for ten years. And she was wanting something more out of life than physical excitement. Money and all that money could buy.

She was just beginning to wonder a little whether it would be rather stupid of her to marry him. If only she could find somebody with more money! Someone like Christopher Fenlick. The young artist had no particular appeal for her, and his cool, rather disdainful attitude towards her infuriated Amanda every time they met. She knew that Christopher saw through her. But it was such a pity the love-affair couldn't have been with him instead of with Jack — or that Jack had his prospects. For Christopher was no starving artist. He was backed by that rich uncle of his, Oscar Fenlick. The old man had a fortune, most of which was tied up in great works of art, but a fortune all the same, and Christopher was his heir.

However, it was no good setting her cap at Mr. Fenlick. She couldn't stand the sententious young fool, anyhow. And there was nobody else with money up at Oxford at the moment who looked like falling for her. So she had better hang on to Jack while she could. He would, of course, make money one day. His uncle's practice was a big one, and security meant something to Amanda, after the very insecure life which she had led since her divorce.

During lunch, she complained bitterly to Jack of most things. She was overworked. Life was lonely and empty when he wasn't up at Oxford. The weather was appalling. It never stopped raining. And so on, until she had got Jack into a state as depressed as her own.

'I know it's all rotten for you, sweet,' he said. 'What you want is a change. You ought to come back to town with me.'

She was silent for a moment, then she said:

'I can't today, but I could over the weekend. Oh, Jack, couldn't we do something exciting in town on Saturday?'

Jack made a few rapid mental calculations and then, hot and embarrassed, admitted that he couldn't afford much.

'I've been overstepping my allowance lately. And my old man is frightfully strict about that sort of thing. So it's no good asking him for an advance.'

Amanda lit a cigarette.

'What about your mother?'

'I can't exactly ask her. She's pretty good to me on the whole, when I really need a helping hand.'

'Oh, well, it doesn't matter,' said Amanda sulkily.

'I wish to God I had some money that I could spend on you,' he said.

'Never mind. We'll do something cheap. I'll pay my share.'

'I hate that.'

'It's customary nowadays.'

'I'll pawn something,' he said. 'I dare say I could raise a bit on my watch, and trust to luck my mother doesn't ask where it is. It's gold. She gave it to me on my last birthday.'

Amanda smiled at him through her long, glistening lashes.

'Aren't you sweet!'

'Promise you'll come, anyhow. It will be marvellous to have you in town.'

'I'll come,' she said.

'Where will you stay?'

She made a little grimace.

'Oh, I have an aunt in Finsbury Park.'

'That doesn't sound your cup of tea, my sweet.'

'It isn't. My cup of tea would have a dash of cognac in it, and we'd have a suite at the Savoy.'

Jack went a little white with the emotion that her words roused in him. His relationship with Amanda was still so new in his life and so wonderful, that he was intoxicated by the mere thought of it. It seemed to him marvellous that this wonderful creature should belong to him. He had the greatest respect for her. Their intimacy had not lessened that respect. He was humble before her. He loathed the thought of that fellow to whom she had been married and who had treated her so shabbily. He wanted to make up to her for all that unhappiness.

'One day, darling, you shall have that suite and a good deal more besides,' he said.

'Meanwhile, I go to Finsbury Park.'

'I wish I could ask you to my home.'

She gave a hard little laugh.

'Can't you see your mother's face if you turned up with me?'

He was silent. He tried to imagine what his mother *would* say if he entered the house with Amanda and asked that she should be accommodated. No doubt Mum would do it, but it wouldn't be a success. He just could not picture Amanda in the bosom of the family. It was this damn business about her having been married and divorced, and being older than himself. Joan would not mind. But the Parents — oh, people of that age were so damned conservative! They'd kick up an awful shindy. They'd say that marriage with Amanda would ruin his life. It was all so senseless. Amanda might be older than he was, but she didn't look it and she was lovely and amusing. Yet if he took home some dull girl from a Vicarage, oozing with virtue, they would be delighted. Of course, the whole fact of the matter was that he could not afford to get married at all for years to come. And that showed how wrong everything was. There was no intelligence in this civilized existence. A man needed a woman in his life when he was young and ardent. And he was expected to lead a celibate existence until he had 'made his way'. The whole system screamed for immorality. Of course, he was singularly lucky to have found an adorable person like Amanda. But he supposed that if his mother or father knew about Amanda, they would say he was leading a shockingly immoral life.

'No, I suppose I'd upset the whole apple-cart if I asked them to put you up at home,' he said.

Amanda, knowing that he was right and justified in what he said, felt perverse today and piqued. She said:

'How much longer am I to be kept a shameful secret from the rest of the Tardys?'

He flushed crimson.

'Don't call yourself a 'shameful secret', for heaven's sake.'

'Well, that's how you make me feel.'

'Mandy! That's not fair! There's nothing shameful about you. I don't think there's anything shameful in our love. You know as well as I do the reason why we've kept it a secret.'

'Well, I think I'm being a bit stupid to let myself be put in such a position and stay in it indefinitely.'

His heart sank. He was used to complaints and grievances from Amanda, but not quite such outspoken discontent. It seemed terrible that she should feel that he, who adored every hair of her head, was responsible for her unhappiness.

Amanda, finished with lunch, made up her face again and ran a comb through her sleek, blonde curls.

'You will admit I'm in a rotten position, Jack darling?'

'Yes,' he said slowly. 'I suppose you are, but I thought we agreed and understood that it couldn't be altered for the moment.'

'Well, it just made me a bit depressed when I was talking to Sheila last night and she told me this man who is interested in her had asked her to marry him. Whilst I — '

'But good God, Mandy!' Jack broke in, 'I *have* asked you to marry me, and you know I'm going to marry you the moment it's possible.'

'Meanwhile, I can't even be taken to your house while I'm in London.'

Jack went a bit pale.

'If you're suggesting that it's just that I don't want to introduce you to my people, I think it's pretty rotten of you. We've discussed the whole business dozens of times. I was under the impression that you agreed that it would be foolish to rush things.'

She did not meet his gaze. She was feeling peevish because she could not get her own way, and life was not really as easy or amusing as it ought to be for a girl with her looks and advantages.

Coldly, she said:

'Oh, quite! I quite agree. Don't let's discuss it further.'

'But if you feel that way about things — '

'Well, it doesn't seem to matter what I feel,' she broke in.

He was aghast. This sort of atmosphere had never really arisen between them before. He could not tolerate the idea that she should be angry or fed-up with him. At the same time, his own personal pride was wounded. He felt that she was being unfair, suddenly to make a bone of contention out of a situation which they had both accepted as inevitable.

Their lunch ended in gloomy silence. Jack called for the bill and paid it. When they stood on the steps outside 'The George', they found that it was still raining. Coming down in a steady, pitiless downpour. Jack swore under his breath.

'I wanted to go out with you somewhere.'

'We'd better go to my place,' said Amanda. 'Sheila won't be back for her next lesson until three and I haven't one till after tea.'

His spirits rose a little.

'Can we be alone for a bit, then?'

'Yes,' she said, without enthusiasm.

He took her arm and they half-walked, half-ran through the rain down the street and into a narrow arcade. Here was the building in which the Deering sisters ran their dancing school. Up a narrow flight of stairs, over a draper's. Outside the front door was a brass plate, with the inscription: *Deering School of Dancing*.

Jack, following Amanda up these familiar stairs which he had climbed innumerable times, touching the highest pinnacle of excitement at the thought of seeing Amanda, wondered what the devil he could do to put things right. He no longer felt cross with her for resenting her position. She had right on her side. It must be most upsetting to her to know that her lover dared not introduce her to his parents. And she was so sweet to him. God! When he thought of the times that he had come up these same stairs and found her waiting for him — what a difference she had made to his life at Oxford — to his whole life, in fact — and what a little he gave her in return! No wonder she complained.

In a reckless mood, he suddenly said:

'I'll tell my mother the whole thing. I'll ask her to see you over the weekend.'

Amanda made no answer. She

unlocked the front door. They passed through into the big, spacious room with the polished floor, which had been converted out of two big attics running right across the top of the building. Some green paint, gay, flame-coloured curtains, one or two mirrors, judicious lighting and flowers went to make an effective *salon* in which the sisters carried on their trade. An electric gramophone and records of all the latest dance-tunes supplied the music.

Since coming here two years ago, Amanda and Sheila had got together a very good business. They were recognized by the colleges, and gave lessons to numbers of undergraduates, as well as to women and men not attached to the colleges. Occasionally they held 'Cinderella Dances' which were always a success.

It was all conducted on business-like lines, and the profits, although small, were steady. The sisters were able to keep themselves and support their father, who had been out of work for years and was a confirmed drunkard.

But there were times when Amanda felt unutterably sick of her existence, could willingly have smashed every record in the *salon* and turned her back on every pupil, with the exception, perhaps, of the best-looking and most attractive of the undergraduates.

Today she felt that everything was wrong — that her whole life had gone awry. She was tired of everything and everybody, even Jack.

Taking off her coat, she flung it on to a chair, hurled her bag after it, switched on the lights and the electric fire, which soon banished the cold and gloom of the April afternoon. Crossing to the gramophone, she switched that on too, and put on a dance record. But almost immediately she turned it off. The music increased her depression. She swung round and faced Jack, who was watching her uneasily and with a pleading look in his eyes which she ignored.

'I shan't come to London at all,' she announced.

'But, darling, I've just said I'd tell my mother about things and introduce you.'

'And have her make a few cracks at me and tell you not to make a fool of yourself. No, thanks! I'm not risking it.'

'I don't think my mother is the sort of woman who makes cracks,' he said stiffly.

'I'm sure she's perfect.'

Jack's eyes flashed.

'Look here, I'm not going to have you — '

'Oh, all right!' she broke in stormily. 'I won't criticize your mother. I don't seem to be able to do or say a thing that's right today. It's a pity you took the trouble to come up to Oxford.'

'It's a pity I did.'

They faced each other, angry, tense, uncomprehending of each other.

Then Jack relented and caught her wrist and drew her into his arms.

'Mandy, sweet. What the hell are we

fighting for? I didn't drive all these miles to have a row with you. I came to tell you how much I adore you. How much I want you. Mandy, don't let's quarrel. It's so stupid. I'm sure my mother would be sweet to you. She's always sweet to everybody and I'll willingly take you home, if you'll just say the word. But you know we've done nothing about it so far because we thought it unwise. We want to get married, don't we? We don't want to make a mess of things. Mandy, say that you *do* want to marry me.'

She thought:

'I suppose it's no good worrying about the money. I'd better take what I can get.'

And there was little doubt that she found the physical thrills that her nature craved in the passionate adoration of this brown, strong, good-looking boy. He was as she liked him to be now, utterly at her feet, pleading for her love, showing how frightened he was of losing her. That

124

gave her a sense of power.

She relaxed in his arms, shut her eyes, and with a little sigh abandoned herself to his caresses.

'Don't mind what I say, Jackie. I was being silly. I know it's wiser not to upset your people. I'll come to town and we'll go out on Saturday night on the cheap and enjoy ourselves.'

He picked her right up in his arms. He liked to do that. He was proud of his strength and equally proud of her slender fragility. He carried her to the sofa in a corner of the room. She could feel his heart pounding madly against her breast.

'I love you! Nothing matters except that. Say it, Mandy.'

She said it with kisses, drawing his head down to hers. Passion engulfed them both, and after that it was very quiet in the Deering School of Dancing. The April rain went on lashing against the windows.

BOOK FOUR

1

Joan Tardy lay in the bath and dreamed impracticable and thrilling dreams which she was almost certain could never possibly come true. But it was nice to dream them, lying in the hot water into which she had just thrown a handful of gardenia bath-salts. (The last handful! There were no more left in the jar which had been given to her a month ago for her birthday.) Bath-salts, good soaps and lovely scents were among the many things which Joan coveted and could not afford out of her allowance.

All today, the thought of that allowance and of the advance which she had not been able to get out of her mother, had rankled within her. She really did hate the idea of turning up at that smart party with the Downes tonight in her old white dress. But she and Gerda had ironed it and managed to make it look fairly presentable. After all, it was a good *crêpe* and well-cut. She had picked it up at a sale in Knightsbridge at Christmas. By way of making a change, she had discarded the ordinary white belt, raked up a few shillings this afternoon, and bought a chiffon scarf of the most heavenly jade green. She was going to put that around her waist. She had a very small waist of which she was proud. And she could wear her jade ear-rings, too. They weren't real, but they looked like it. She had small white ears set well back. Anthony had told her at the Metfords' the other night that she was the type to wear ear-rings because of her nice little ears and well-shaped head.

Of course, if she believed half that Anthony Downe said to her, she would come to the conclusion that she had the most divine figure in London. He had been so flattering the other night. And Agatha Downe had told her that Brother Tony was intrigued by her. (An awful woman, Agatha, but frightfully smart and clever. Only Joan wished she wouldn't be quite so theatrical. She supposed that it was all part of her make-up as a dress-designer. All those superlatives she used and that gush . . . no doubt it was useful in her trade, but frightful to listen to.)

Anthony had said that she, Joan, was not too tall. Just perfect, and she moved well. Any time she wanted a job as a mannequin he'd give her one. That was a pretty big offer. There must be hundreds of girls who'd like to be mannequins for Anthony Downe. But not Joan. She was much too self-conscious. She couldn't imagine herself swaying across a platform in front of people, showing off clothes — even though they were Anthony or Agatha's marvellous creations.

And what a showroom they had! Joan had been greatly impressed the first day she had attended a Dress Show there, when the spring models were being displayed. Those two rooms in Berkeley

Square must have cost thousands to convert and decorate. There was a little stage with a cream velvet background against which the dresses looked marvellous. A crowd of chic people were present. Anthony Downe had a large *clientèle*. He specialized in suits and evening things. The prices of them made Joan gasp. One of those velvet evening coats displayed, trimmed with silver-fox, cost three times more than two years of her allowance!

It seemed so queer that there should be such a difference in the various ways in which people lived. When Joan sat down in the Downes' smart show-rooms, amongst all those well-dressed women, she felt shabby and a nobody. Yet she was a doctor's daughter, and she knew that there were thousands of girls much worse off, who would give anything to be in her place. Everything was relative.

At the same time, nothing had annoyed Joan more than the old adage which relations liked to quote, about

'Think how much luckier you are than So-and-so.' Just as they said when you were small: 'Eat up this or that. Think how many poor starving children there are who would give anything to have your food!' To which Joan had always felt like answering: 'Let them have it.'

There were times when she was ashamed of her discontent. After all, she had a good, comfortable home and she adored the family. She admired Mummy frightfully, too, only sometimes they didn't get on because they didn't understand each other too well. Mummy was just a bit old-fashioned, poor darling. As for Daddy, he was an old pet! Too sweet — rushing round at his job — hardly ever home. Joan didn't really feel that she knew her father well. To Jack, she was devoted. She was proud of his good looks and his obvious attraction for her girlfriends. They all fell for Jack. He was amusing and friendly with them, but so far he had never shown any signs of being really intrigued. Joan had a secret belief that he had a girlfriend up at Oxford. She meant to try to get him to tell her about it some time. As for Mogs — well, she was just a kid, and a bit of a nuisance at the moment. Joan hoped Mogs would get better-looking with time. She was so appallingly fat and ungainly at the moment. And so exacting! When she first came back from school, she always complained that Joan didn't pay any attention to her and she had only *just* got home. And before long, she was saying that Joan ought to take her out, or play cards with her because she was *just* going back to school! There was scarcely a time when Mogs didn't expect some particular attention.

Lying in her bath luxuriating, Joan's thoughts were, however, not on the family this evening. They were with Anthony Downe. Her dreams were taking him and herself in Anthony's beautiful black and silver car down the Corniche Road, heading for Monte Carlo. There, in the drenching sun, with the burning blue skies and the burning blue sea and all the glamour of the Mediterranean coast, Joan would learn to *Live*. As Anthony Downe had lived.

The last time they had met, he had talked to her about his trips to the French Riviera. He had said how necessary it was for her to experience the beauty and glamour of it. And Joan, who had been strictly and sedately brought up at home and at St. Brede's, now badly wanted to 'break out'.

The first time she had even begun to see or feel what life could mean had been at school in Lausanne, where she had had a brief but delicious passion for her ski-ing instructor. There could be quite a lot of glamour about a good-looking young man on skis, in the sparkling mountain air. Then that had finished. They had exchanged longing glances, one or two notes and an ardent pressure of the hand. That was all. After which Joan had come back home and done nothing in particular, until she met Anthony Downe.

In two short meetings, Anthony had

proved to Joan that she was wasting her time and her life. He had made her see how dull existence was in this house with the family. She longed passionately to get away from any kind of control and find herself in a flat of her own, where she could live as the Downes and their friends lived. Where she could get up at any hour she liked and go to bed when she wanted. Have someone to wait on her hand and foot, pick up her clothes when she dropped them, mend all her stockings (or better still, be able to afford a new pair if the old ones laddered). Eat what she wanted, drink what she wanted without criticism. In fact, be *herself* and not the Joan whom the family wished her to be.

Of course, all those dreams about Anthony and the Mediterranean were absurd. What really faced her was three weeks in some frightful, second-rate hotel in England. The family holiday again!

Gloomily, Joan looked up at the ceiling. It was cracked and the paper was peeling off. The bath in which she was lying was of the big, old fashioned type. Red stains ran down the porcelain, relics of a dripping tap. It had mahogany sides which were badly in need of repair. Everything in this house was out of date, Joan thought. Mummy recognized the fact and wanted to modernize the rooms. But the trouble was, Daddy never had enough money.

Joan had a moment's vision of the bathroom in the Downes' flat. Agatha had shown her over it yesterday. *What* a room! A glass floor, black sunken bath, and strip lighting which made everything glow with a diffused gold radiance. Every sort of spray and shower. Rows of coloured crystal bottles containing expensive bath essences and lotions. Great, soft, coloured towels over the hot rails. *Luxury!*

Joan was begging to believe that she should have been born into a millionaire's family. She did love expensive things so terribly. And here she was, about to step out into a cold, unheated bathroom and dry herself with a small, rough towel which was patched and grey from much washing. The only decent towels they had in this house were kept for visitors. It was the same with the sheets. There were some lovely new, coloured, linen ones which Mummy had bought at a sale, but they went into Daddy's and her room. The rest of the family used up the old school cotton and twill! She would remind Mummy that she had *promised* to get her linen ones this summer, pale green, to match her room.

It was mean of her to turn up her nose too much, because Mummy had done up her room quite nicely for her. She couldn't complain about that. But of course it couldn't compare with a room like Agatha Downe's. She couldn't forget Agatha's room. That lovely double divan with a canopy of brilliant blue figured silk. Silver walls and ceiling. Gorgeous curtains of blue and silver brocade. Joan had only just peeped at it when she was at the flat yesterday.

Suddenly the handle of the bathroom door was rattled. Came Jack's voice:

'Joan! Are you still in there? For God's sake hurry up. I want a bath.'

Joan sat up, brought back with a thud to earth.

'I didn't know you were home,' she called.

'Just got back. We had the car open, and I'm drenched and cold.'

Joan, feeling in a good humour because of the thrilling evening which she was about to have, climbed out of the bath and seized her towel.

'I won't be long. Did you have a good time?'

'No, lousy!'

'Why?'

No answer. Jack had gone. Joan, rubbing her slim white body vigorously, nodded to herself. Jack always came back in an ill humour from these expeditions to Oxford. She was certain that there was some girl up there who attracted him and that things weren't going too well for the old boy.

Somebody else shook the handle of the door.

'All right! All right!' called Joan. 'I'm just coming.'

Came her mother's sweet, rather low voice:

'Aren't you rather late, darling? You said you wanted to be at your party by half-past seven. It's nearly seven now.'

'Oh, God!' exploded Joan.

'Darling!' The endearment was said in terms of reproof. Clare did not like the children to use their Maker's name quite so often and so unnecessarily as they did.

Joan was out of the bathroom with great rapidity. In the bedroom, Clare waited to help her dress. She liked to do this, but as a rule Joan turned everybody out. Tonight, however, she accepted her mother's attentions gladly. She had lain in that bath much longer than she had intended. Anthony had told her not to be late because they were dining early. The show was to begin at eight-thirty.

Clare had Joan's best pair of stockings and her silver shoes waiting for her. Flushed and breathless, Joan slid into a pair of diminutive pink silk pants and a pink brassière.

Clare looked anxiously at the girl while she slipped the white dress over her head.

'Darling, don't you wear anything else? I'm sure you'll catch cold. It's quite chilly tonight.'

Joan answered crossly:

'Don't be silly, Mum. We always have that argument. You know I never wear much.'

Clare sighed. She knew. And she could never accustom herself to the idea that so little should be worn in the winter as well as the summer. These girls never seemed to catch cold. That was one blessing. Clare almost envied Joan being able to do with a yard or two of silk like that. She, herself, could not bear going through damp, chilly weather without woollies. Joan had not worn a vest since she had come back from Lausanne, when she had discarded all her wool undergarments and passed them on to Mogs. Such fads were catching, too. Mogs had actually started to complain about having to wear combinations. But Clare intended to be quite firm with Mogs.

At last Joan, complete, stood before her mirror, and regarded herself. Her mother thought that she looked lovely. Joan thought so too and hoped that Anthony would agree. The white dress was tight-fitting, accentuating the lines of her slim hips and small waist. That green sash was an inspiration. So were the ear-rings. They brought out the greeny tints in her eyes. She had bought a box of eyelid shadow today. She leaned closer to the mirror and rubbed a little of the blue-black cream on her lids. Her mother watched this performance a trifle critically.

'I don't think that's necessary, Joan. It gives you a terribly artificial look, darling. You're quite pretty enough without it.'

'No, I'm not. It adds glamour.'

Clare opened her mouth to say more, but Joan had not time to listen. She seized her evening coat (silver brocade with fur cuffs and *quite* done, but it was all she had), pressed a quick kiss on her mother's cheek and dashed down the stairs.

Her mother's voice followed her.

'Have you got your latch-key?'

'Hell, no!'

The key was thrown over the banisters.

'*Do* moderate your language, darling.'

But Joan was not out to moderate anything. She was sick of moderation — and the family. She wanted to have a really good time and she meant to have it — tonight.

She could not afford a taxi to Berkeley Square, where the Downes lived. She had intended taking a bus as far as Berkeley Street, then walking.

She was dismayed to find that it was raining hard.

That meant a two-shilling taxi. She could ill afford it. Damn her allowance! She stood hesitant. Then her father's car drove up. Never had Joan been more thankful to see the shabby blue saloon which the family called 'The Tortoise', because it crawled. Dr. Tardy stepped out of the car with his bag. She waved and yelled at him.

'Hi! Pop! Be a saint and drive me to my party. It's such a ghastly night.'

Dr. Tardy, with an air of resignation, put his case back into the car and took his place at the wheel again.

Joan ran through the rain, dived into The Tortoise, and slammed the door.

'What a piece of luck, catching you.'

'Maybe a bit of luck for you, but not for me,' he said good-humouredly. 'I've got some more work to do, young lady. W.O.R.K. You don't know what that means.'

She grimaced and laughed.

'Now, Pop. No lectures. I'm in a party mood.'

He looked down at her. The child looked radiant and pretty, but he didn't like all that stuff on her face. However, he had long since grown tired of telling her so. He took out a handkerchief and wiped his glasses.

'Hurry, darling,' said Joan. 'I'm so late already.'

They started to move down the wet, shining street. It was blowing hard as well as raining. There was a traffic block just beyond Harrods. Dr. Tardy never took any risks. No cutting in and out of the traffic with cunning dexterity like Anthony Downe. Joan sighed and strove to be patient. After all, she was lucky to be driven to Berkeley Square, if only in The Tortoise.

'Who do you know in Berkeley Square?' her father was asking.

She explained.

Dr. Tardy wrinkled his nose.

'Never heard of the Downes.'

'Of course you haven't. Doctors

145

don't deal with dress-designers, unless they are taking out their tonsils, or something.'

'Where did you meet them?'

'At the Metfords'.'

'Ah, yes!'

Joan smiled to herself. She knew that tone of Daddy's. He was satisfied because the Metfords were patients and acquaintances of his and Mummy's. How narrow the old people were. They could never, with complete satisfaction, accept anybody or anything outside their own circle.

Dr. Tardy said:

'Don't much care for young men who design dresses. Silly sort of job for a man.'

'Dress-designers are not necessarily 'pansies', darling.'

'I don't know what you mean by 'pansies', dear,' said Dr. Tardy blandly.

Joan put her tongue in her cheek. He understood all right. But he wasn't going to admit it. She added:

'Well, they're not necessarily effeminate. Look what famous ones there are! In fact, all the most famous dress-designers are men, and more and more are taking it up. It's no more effeminate than being an artist, like Jack's friend Christopher.'

'Oh, I don't know. Hanging round women all day, draping 'em in bits of stuff — that sort of thing — '

'Well, Anthony Downe is very nice, anyhow. And *very* much a man.'

'Good!' said Dr. Tardy.

He had ceased to be interested in his daughter's friends. He was wondering whether he ought to get Sir Robert Cunningham to see that Mitchell child. There was a definite throat infection. But of course one could wait until morning, without undue risk, and see what developed. He didn't want to put the Mitchells to the expense of a specialist unless it was necessary. They were hard-up.

Joan's high, clear young voice cut in on his thoughts.

'I'm going to the new revue, Pops. My first 'First Night'. Isn't it thrilling?'

'If you like that sort of thing, I suppose it is.'

'Well, darling. We can't *all* like Promenade Concerts at the Queen's Hall, can we?'

'I think that people who prefer revue to a really good concert definitely lose something, and quite definitely gain nothing.'

'I'd love to take you out one night, Daddy, and make you do all the sort of things I do. Go places and see things, and watch the effect on you.'

'Nothing doing, young lady. I'd as soon take an anæsthetic as have the sort of night-out you'd prescribe.'

Joan was silent after that. She wondered whether it would be nice to be so settled in one's mind. So conservative in one's ideas, and so placid as her father. No doubt it saved one a lot of trouble. Daddy seemed very happy. But at the moment, Joan felt that she would prefer the 'divine discontent' which she was experiencing. She was going to fall in love with Anthony Downe. She knew it. She knew that if he looked at her and talked to her as he had done the other day, or said things like he had said on the 'phone this morning, she would never be able to keep calm and collected.

It was the first time she had ever been so affected. One or two men in these last few months had tried to make her interested in them. That conceited fool, Christopher Fenlick, whom she couldn't bear, was always wanting her to go and sit for him, and had made a lot of remarks about her figure which hadn't thrilled her at all. Neither had that boy, Derek Smith-Jones, who had taken her out last weekend to a show and a dance, amused her. In fact, she did not like young men. She preferred the older ones. They were so much easier to talk to. Much more attractive in every way. She began to feel wildly excited at the thought of this evening and Anthony Downe.

2

The evening came up to Joan's expectations. She had felt excited at the prospect of it and she was not disappointed when at length she found herself in the Downes' flat. There were four of them for dinner. Joan, Anthony Downe, his sister Agatha and an effete young man with fair wavy hair, a high forehead and an agonized expression. His full name, Joan never really found out. Agatha called him 'Pony'. She said he looked like one. He kept shaking his head and making his long hair fly wildly, like a pony tossing its mane. Agatha assured Joan that he 'stamped his hoof' when he was impatient.

He wrote poetry. He had published one book of verses, which sold four copies. Just now he appeared to be looking for a job which nobody would give him.

How he lived, Joan had no idea, but Agatha said that he was always 'everywhere'. He wore exquisite 'tails', a deep navy blue, a white carnation in his buttonhole and a monocle, which partly accounted for the anguish of his screwed-up face when he stuck the glass in his eye.

Pony appeared to be Agatha's attendant-in-chief. Anthony said that he adored her and had dedicated his book of poems to her. Joan thought him rather ludicrous and imagined how Mogs would giggle if she saw him. Joan wondered how Agatha could endure him. She was so much older and more sensible. She supposed Agatha was flattered by his attentions. Joan did not pretend to be clever, but she came to the conclusion quickly that she had never heard anybody let forth a stream of more arrant nonsense at a greater speed than Pony. Agatha Downe managed to keep pace with him, however. They both laughed a great deal at innuendos which were lost upon Joan. She was quite dazed by the rapidity and hidden meaning in all the smart repartee during the evening.

Anthony could keep pace with it and did so when he bothered his head. But he was concentrating upon Joan and behaved as though he did not really want to see anybody else. He made Joan feel at once that she was the one person for whom he had been looking all his life.

She felt that he was being just kind when he praised her dress. She knew that he must secretly think it was awful, and she told him so.

'An expert like you, Mr. Downe — you're just laughing at me!'

'Sweet infant, for heaven's sake call me Anthony,' was his reply. 'And believe me when I tell you that I think your little white dress is charming. But one day . . . ah! . . . I shall design something that is really *You!*

Dazzled, Joan sat on the arm of the sofa in the drawing-room, sipping her cocktail. She had no idea what was in it, but it was very strong, and she came to the conclusion that she had better not drink it all.

Everything was wonderful tonight. Anthony. Life! This all-white room. Even the covers and curtains were white — some thick, creamy, brocaded material. Cream walls. And — Joan wondered what they would say at home to the carpet — that too was cream. Wanton extravagance! Before the fireplace was a scarlet rug. And there were great, white, shimmering cushions edged with scarlet. Scarlet carnations flaunting their heads from a tall vase by the window. At one end of the room, an ebony baby grand with the lid open and a lot of music on it. Anthony played. And composed. Not the classics that Joan's father loved. But dance-music. Clever little songs.

There were one or two glass tables, a silver painted cocktail cabinet and a radio-gramophone. The sound came through a black wrought-iron grille, as though out of the wall. Agatha turned on the wireless and kept music playing all the time they were there, as a background to the chatter.

Agatha, Joan thought, fitted in with the room. Sleek black head, close-cropped. A dead white face. Her red dress fitted her tall, thin figure like a glove. She wore long diamond ear-rings. She looked feverish, burnt up with the force of her own physical energy. So far as Joan could see, she was never still for five minutes. Never had a cigarette or a drink out of her hand. Joan tried to imagine her mother meeting and liking Agatha Downe, and failed. There could not be much difference in their ages — Agatha Downe must be nearing forty — yet they might have been of different generations.

Anthony had a look of his sister. He, too, was thin and white, with a feverish intensity about him. He was a little shorter, for Agatha was a tall woman, but he was gracefully built and moved so beautifully that he did not strike Joan as being short. He was ten years younger than Agatha — but there was nothing young about his face. It was sculptured in the classic sense and incredibly old. Joan could not imagine that he had ever been young, nor could she begin to guess what lay behind those dark, long-lashed, brilliant eyes of his. When he smiled, it made her think of the words which Oscar Wilde might have applied to that smile . . . 'curved . . . archaic' . . . and immensely exciting. Certainly Anthony had an exciting quality. But he was less energetic than Agatha. He had a lazy, exhausted way of speaking and moving. His were the hands of an artist — with long, slender fingers.

Joan could so well imagine him handling all the lovely fabrics with which he created his dresses. His fingers would caress the soft silks, the rich velvets, the smooth satins, as they would caress a woman's hair or shoulders. Delicately, sensuously. They had a very disturbing effect upon Joan when he touched her for an instant to draw her attention to something in the room.

'So you'll design a dress for me, one day, will you, Anthony?' she said, using his name a trifle shyly.

His gaze travelled over her with satisfaction. Anthony Downe knew a perfect figure when he saw one. He raised his cocktail glass, looked at her over it, and said:

'To Beauty unadorned. There is nothing I could do to make you more beautiful.'

She gave a little laugh. The warm colour high in her cheeks.

'Don't be so ridiculous.'

He smiled.

'Then I'll dress you in a sheath of silver, with a coat of mail, and you shall be Joan of Arc, the fair maid who led France to her doom.'

'To victory, surely,' said Joan.

'You could lead men to either.'

Joan had to think a moment before that penetrated into her mind. She never could make her brain work as quickly as she wanted. She was sure she missed the full significance of half the things the Downes said to her and each other. But she could not be unaware of Anthony's flattery. She sipped her own drink and her lids drooped a little before the ardour in his eyes. She said:

'I could never lead anybody to anything. I'd much rather be led.'

'Divine! I'll be your leader. Where shall I take you? To the end of the world?'

'That's a long way.'

'Not long enough.'

Agatha Downe, conversing with her poet, caught that last remark, turned her smooth black head, and laughed over her shoulder:

'Is Tony saying nice things to you, Joan?'

'Very nice,' said Joan.

'Then you can believe them,' said Agatha, 'because he's quite sober at this early hour.'

'You can believe what I say when I'm not sober,' said Anthony, and walked to the cocktail cabinet to refill his glass. 'I always stick to the truth, even when in a state of intoxication.'

Pony followed him, eyeing Joan.

'Take my advice,' he said, 'and never believe anything that either Agatha or Tony say to you, unless it's insulting.'

'God!' said Agatha Downe. 'Listen to the man. He's *obviously* sober. Give him a strong drink, Tony. What about another for you, Joan?'

She shook her head.

'I haven't finished this one yet.'

Agatha Downe handed in her glass. She was a little bored by Joan. She was always bored by the young and ignorant. She was not quite sure why brother Anthony was interesting himself in the child. A doctor's daughter with dull, sticky parents, according to Barbara Metford who was one of Anthony's clients. Of course, Joan was extremely pretty. But that white dress with the green sash was pathetic. Perhaps Tony just wanted 'fun and games' with her. But as a rule he didn't choose her type. He liked a more *soignèe* woman. And he was still in the teeth of a storm over Veronica Porteous.

Tony had been busy making clothes for the lovely Lady Porteous for the last twelve months. Equally busy making a lot of trouble between her and her husband. There'd nearly been a suit about it. But Bill Porteous didn't want a scandal because of their little girl, and he'd done the big forgiving act and taken Veronica back to the fold. She was still writing frantic letters to Tony. Tony didn't want to be involved in a divorce. He had for a time been more than usually in love with Veronica, who was a lovely, decadent creature. But he felt that she was better suited to be a man's mistress than his wife. Added to which, Anthony Downe was not a marrying man.

Agatha knew that Tony was tired of Veronica and her neurosis. She presumed that he was in the mood to interest himself in a sweet young thing with ideals. He would get 'a kick' out of disillusioning her.

Anthony Downe, for the moment however, had no intention of disillusioning Joan Tardy. It was not only her physical appeal but her personality which attracted him. She was neither silly nor boring. There was something frank and genuine about her which he found refreshing after the women whom usually he made his friends. God knew, he was sick of Veronica Porteous. If she made him one scene, she made him twenty. That week at Cap Martin had been glorious but quite devitalizing. Being Veronica's lover meant that one could never relax. He had always to be at the top of his form in order to amuse and satisfy her. He had never known a woman more *exigeante*. He had had to drink a lot, too, to keep up to the high pitch of excitement required. Exciting though it was, escorting the lovely Lady Porteous here, there and everywhere (the scandal was part of the excitement for Anthony, for it was more essential that he should have the reputation for being the best designer of clothes than the guardian of a husband's morals) it had almost ruined him. One could spend packets of money on Veronica and be made to feel that one had spent nothing.

How tired he had been! Tired, the whole time their affair continued. Veronica was so analytical. She would analyse their passion, dissect it into fragments, examine every bit, hold *post mortems* on past sensations, as well as devise new ones, until he was quite worn out.

He remembered one night when they had quarrelled over some minor jealously, made it up, passionately in each other's arms, then started quarrelling again almost as soon as they began to talk once more. In the early hours of the morning, regretting the harsh words she had spoken, Veronica had drawn him back to her lips and called him 'her lovely, cruel, Marcus Antonius'. Whereupon he, mentally and physically shattered, flung himself at her feet and quoted with more honesty than irony:

"I am dying, Egypt!"

This evening, Anthony Downe banished the visions of his turbulent and exotic interlude with Veronica Porteous and felt that he would like to spend a long time with this slender, attractive child, Joan. He liked her red-brown coronet of curls, and her calm, sedate little manner. She was cool and restful . . . like spring water, he told himself . . . like morning dew . . . like a bird. He must ask Pony to write a poem about her and he would set it to music. But no, she wasn't bird-like — she was more soothing. Birds were twittering things. Definitely, Joan soothed him. He did not want to do her any harm. But he would like to lie on a sofa and let her hold his hand and stroke his hair and say something quaint and honest, so that he could smile — it was such a delight to get away from the lure or sting or double-meaning in Veronica's words. What the hell he was going to do with Veronica, he didn't know. It wasn't enough for her that she should have been on the verge of divorce and that Lord Porteous should have given her another chance. She was trying to see him, Anthony, again. He had had a letter from her this evening, saying:

'I don't think I can tolerate living with a selfrighteous idiot who does nothing but remind me that I have sinned and that he has pardoned me. Oh, Marcus Antonius, can't we meet again? . . . ' She had signed it: *'Egypt'*.

But Anthony Downe no longer felt that he was 'dying' so far as Veronica Porteous was concerned. He was dead. And if she wasn't going to be sensible about this business, she might make things very awkward for him. Especially if she let Bill think that they were starting the affair all over again.

Looking at Joan and that young, unkissed mouth of hers, he thought:

'I wish to God dear Egypt would get an asp and put the proper finish to it. I'm terribly, *terribly* tired, and only this

163

young, cool creature can give me rest.'

To Joan he said:

'Your hair is a melody in itself. It's neither red, nor brown, but both. Like the brush of a fox. Ah! That's what I shall call you. Little Fox!'

'Not a vixen, I hope.'

He swept that aside with one slim, sensitive hand.

'The very reverse. You could never be malicious or cruel. I can imagine you would always be kind. But because of your hair, I shall call you Little Fox.'

Joan's eyes sparkled.

'That's rather an amusing name.'

At once, Anthony had to draw the others into the conversation in order to get the full dramatic effect. Above all things, he enjoyed making an effect.

'Agatha! Pony! I've got a wonderful name for Joan. I'm going to call her Little Fox, because of her hair.'

'Are you the hound in full cry?' asked Agatha, with a touch of sarcasm.

That made Joan feel hot and rather uncomfortable, but Anthony laughed.

'Darling! *Am* I hound-like? I haven't enough energy to leap across this room in pursuit of anything — even such an entrancing fox as this one — ' he waved a hand in Joan's direction.

'I call that *immensely* clever,' put in Pony. 'May I write a verse to the Little Fox? So intriguing!'

'I hoped you would,' said Anthony. 'And I'll do the music for it. It would make a superb number for a revue.'

'I think you're terribly clever,' said Joan to Anthony, 'being able to write music as well as design all those lovely dresses.'

Agatha put in:

'Talking of revue, we shall be late for ours if we don't have our food now.'

Laughing and talking, they moved into the dining-room. This also was white. Black and white striped curtains. A black glass table around which were narrow chairs with enormously tall brocaded backs. On the table, lighted by six candles in gilt candelabra, was set what Agatha called a 'little theatre dinner'. A variety of exquisitely served cold foods. Joan thought she had never seen a more fascinating sight than the pale pink salmon, cool green cucumber, quails in aspic and a multi-coloured salad in a white china bowl — all set upon the black glass. Two slim bottles of hock had been iced and a man-servant in a white coat opened them and poured the pale liquid into tall Venetian glasses.

For a moment Joan had a vision of her home. The family gathered round the old-fashioned mahogany table on which the mats would be slightly soiled, because they only had clean ones once a week. There would be a loaf of bread and some cold, hard toast. Tonight there'd probably be cold joint (they'd had a hot one for lunch), and one of Lucy's treacle-puddings. Joan shuddered. Anthony and Agatha Downe would think such food plebeian and revolting.

She took the glass of hock which Anthony handed her. He clinked his glass against hers and whispered:

'To the Little Fox.'

'To the hound,' she said, trying to be clever and afterwards feeling that she had issued a direct invitation which made her horribly embarrassed. But Anthony laughed and whispered again:

'If I catch you, I promise I shan't tear you to pieces. I'll come and sit in your lair and wag my tail, which would be the most unorthodox end to any hunt.'

Her embarrassment lifted. He had such a way of making one feel at one's ease. The dinner was most exciting.

3

The First Night of the new revue, 'Keep Singing', was exciting too. The Downes had been given a box. Anthony knew the woman who had dressed the show. It was the first time Joan had ever been in a box. She felt very grand and superior, looking down upon the stalls.

She remembered the last time she had come to this particular theatre to see John Gielgud, who had always been her favourite actor. She had stood in a queue with Mogs, who had forsaken Ivor Novello to please Joan. Then they had got two seats at the back of the pit. But *this* was marvellous, in this box with these amusing friends who seemed to know everybody who came into the theatre. That was, everybody of note.

It was very pleasant to have Anthony sitting so close to her, pointing out all the exciting people, and to feel his hand now and again brush lightly across her bare shoulder. Pony, monocle in eye, stood just behind Agatha, passing gloomy comments. He seemed to Joan of a lachrymose disposition. His poetic soul would not allow him to laugh or do more than smile sorrowfully at Agatha's jokes. But he kept assuring everybody that he was having 'the most divine evening'.

The revue itself was a brilliant, frothy affair. There were a lot of lovely girls wearing as little as possible. Some superlative dancing. Several sentimental duets by a favourite leading lady and a handsome hero. And one good dance number which was plugged by the orchestra all the way through the show. Joan sang it under her breath and was gratified when Anthony whispered that 'she must have a good ear', and that he would make her sing to him one day.

Joan was not the musical member of her family, but on the few occasions when she had attempted to sing at home, her efforts had been received with such derision from her brother and sister that she had attempted it no more. She reflected tonight that it seemed pathetic one should only be appreciated by people outside one's own home.

The intervals were the highlights of the evening. Agatha and Pony went off in one direction and Joan and Anthony walked through the bar and foyer where Anthony was greeted by so many people whom he introduced to Joan that she lost count of them. But she remembered the most thrilling ones. What a lot she would have to pour out at the breakfast-table to Jack and Mogs! She met a well-known newspaper critic. A famous Viennese actress. A gentleman with a pointed beard who, Anthony told her, was the portrait painter of the day. Two members of Anthony's own profession.

Anthony appeared to be a great favourite. He was hailed here, there and everywhere as 'Tony, old boy', called 'my dear' by a golden-haired youth whom Joan detested at sight but who Anthony said was a creator of *divine* hats, and greeted as 'darling' richly and breathlessly by half a dozen well-dressed, well-painted women.

It was all a revelation to Joan. It gave her a terrific thrill being Anthony Downe's companion, and to feel herself envied as such. And it was so far removed from her normal life. She began to think of her mother and father with pity. Jack, of course, had a great time up at Oxford and would probably extract the same 'kick' out of tonight as she did. But poor Mum and Pop — how out of their depth they'd be in the Downes' circle and how little they could appreciate it at its true value. Joan was quite shocked when she returned to the box to hear Agatha complaining. She said:

'I think it's rather a yawn-making show. There isn't a soul in the theatre I want to talk to. Let's go on to the Coconut Grove and dance.'

But Anthony had other plans.

'You and Pony can go to the Coconut. I think the Little Fox should be taken home.'

'Oh, no — ' began Joan breathlessly.

His fingers closed around her wrist with a warning pressure. He whispered:

'I've other plans for us.'

She kept silent. Her heart beat faster. There was something so intimate and significant in his touch and his voice.

'Keep Singing' ended as a First Night should end. In rapturous applause, the curtain going up and down and up and down. Stars and producer taking their bows. Calls and cheers from the gallery. Speeches.

Finally, they moved out through the crush in the theatre to the strains of the dance-tune which Anthony said was going to be a 'hit number'. Joan said:

'It's a big success, isn't it?'

'I doubt it. Only one decent tune.'

'But the audience seemed so pleased.'

'They're always like that for a

production of Ducayne's. You never can tell. It may run a week. It may run six months.'

Joan listened reverently. How wonderful to know everything, to be sure of oneself. It did make her feel such a suburban little fool.

Agatha and Pony bade Joan 'good night' and departed to their dance club. Anthony took Joan's arm as they came out into the street where the theatre crowd dispersed. They walked a little way before they hailed a taxi. The rain had stopped. It was cool and fresh, and warmer. And there were stars out. Stars that looked very far away and pale. Joan looked up at them and shivered nervously. After her tremendous evening, she was keyed up to a high pitch of excitement.

When Anthony Downe suggested that they might go back to his flat for a drink before he took her home, her first instinct was to say 'yes'. Her next instinct was born of principles, all the barriers of convention with which she had been surrounded since her birth.

'I don't know that I ought to — ' she began.

'My dear Little Fox,' he cut in, laughing gently, 'the hound isn't in such full cry as all that. There's nothing for you to be afraid of. I've already told you I shan't eat you up.'

She crimsoned. Her eyes were bright and shy.

'Oh, I know that — '

'Would you rather I took you straight home?'

Of course she wouldn't. She wanted very much to go back to his flat and sit with him for a while. She had never been more disturbed or enthralled by anybody in her life. And why not go? Why stand here hesitating when she had told herself for weeks now that she wanted to live her own life? She could begin to live it tonight. She needn't tell the family that she had gone back to Anthony's flat. And it was being frightfully stupid and out-of-date to turn down such an invitation. Of course, Mum would take it for granted that if a girl went back to a man's flat, she was ruined. Joan wanted to prove to Anthony that she was neither stupid nor old-fashioned.

'Of course I'll come back with you,' she said breathlessly.

In the taxi going to Berkeley Square, his hand found hers and held it:

'Enjoyed yourself?'

'It's been marvellous.'

'For me, too. A very pleasant change to take somebody out who isn't bored or blasé. I love to watch your expressions and hear all your funny little opinions.'

Joan pouted.

'Are they so funny?'

'Delicious! But you are a most delicious person. I told you that before.'

Her excitement intensified. His hand was now resting on her knee. She could feel the warmth of it through the thin white *crêpe* of her dress. The colour left her face. She had never before experienced physical emotion like this about any man. She decided there and then that she was in love. Yes, she had fallen frightfully in love with Anthony Downe. Had he taken her in his arms at that moment, she would willingly have lifted her lips for his kisses. But Anthony Downe was not the man to hurry things. When he found anything good, he liked to savour it slowly. 'Rush a dress through and it will never look right' was his motto in his business. Rush a love-affair and that would be equally a mistake. He was going to have a love-affair with this pretty child. But he would approach it slowly, cautiously, and make perfectly certain that at the moment when he really wanted her youth and sweetness, they would be his for the asking.

He kept his hand on her knee until the taxi slowed down and they approached the block of flats in Berkeley Square. Then, for an instant, he touched her red-brown coronet of curls and said:

'Aren't you the sweetest Fox?'

She found no answer. But as she went with him through the luxurious, lighted hall and into the lift which took them up smoothly and swiftly to the Downes' penthouse, her mind worked somewhat deliriously. She supposed that she was being frightfully wicked going up to a man's flat alone at this time of night, and that the family would be shocked beyond words to see her and to hear how unprotestingly she accepted all the things that Anthony said to her. She could well imagine how, if she told her mother that she had fallen in love with him, she would say:

'You're *much* too young to think of being in love.'

Jack and Mogs would jeer. And her father would pass some vague, caustic comment and say no more about it.

Oh, she was going to take good care not to tell the family a *word* about this. They were too unsympathetic. Of course they didn't mean to be. They were darlings, really. But they didn't *understand*. Didn't understand that she was no longer the Joan Tardy of their imagination. She was another Joan who belonged to herself.

She had a great friend who had been at Lausanne with her, Pamela Edison. She might tell Pam about it, but she'd be the only one. And it would have to wait, because Pam lived in Shropshire and she wouldn't want to write about anything as important and secret as this. But Pam was coming up to town next week, and she could pour it all out to her then.

The moment they were in the flat, Anthony seated himself at the piano and began to play. Joan took off her coat and sat in an armchair from where she could see him. She had never felt a deeper satisfaction than resting silently there in that white, beautiful room — in darkness except for the orange glow of the electric fire, and one lamp in a huge glass bowl which threw its light upon the piano. And the sight of Anthony Downe's slim, graceful figure sitting there, black tails spread behind him over the piano-stool, sensitive hands hovering over the keyboard, inscrutable eyes turned in her direction while he played. And how perfectly he played! Enchanting little dance-tunes. Fragments of insinuating songs, humming the words in his low, lazy voice.

He began to improvise:

'*Little Fox with the red-brown
    hair,*
I'm looking for you everywhere,
I'm all forlorn.
Little Fox, sweet Little Fox,
Where have you gone?'

She gave a delighted little laugh and murmured:

'Fancy thinking of that all in a minute!'

He rose from the stool, moved to the corner cabinet and pulled out drinks. Joan wouldn't have one. He poured himself out a whisky and soda and came and sat on the arm of her chair.

'*Little Fox with the red-brown hair,*'

he quoted and began to play with her curls.

Her heart seemed to tumble over and she sat quite still, as though not daring to move.

He saw that her hands were shaking. He was quite touched to note the effect he was having upon her. It had taken half a dozen drinks and a good deal more besides to make Veronica tremble for him. Really! He was beginning to think that virginal charm was the greatest, and the untutored mind the most exciting for a man to explore.

He said:

'I suppose you have dozens of hounds in full cry after you, haven't you?'

'If you mean boyfriends — none,' she laughed. 'I don't like boys.'

'Only old gentlemen like me?'

'You can hardly call yourself that.'

'As a matter of fact, I'm quite heart-broken at your insinuation that I'm not 'just a boy'!'

She looked at him anxiously, and

found that he was laughing at her. He added:

'As a matter of fact, very young men can be frightfully boring. You've got a brother, haven't you?'

'Yes. But Jack's awfully nice. He's the most interesting member of my family, I think.'

'No. You are.'

'I'm not at all interesting, really.'

'I shall argue that point with you, but not now. Tell me more about your brother.'

'He's at Oxford.'

Anthony raised his brows and surveyed his drink thoughtfully.

'He's lucky. At his age I was learning to design clothes in Paris.'

'Well, you've made a big success, and for all that Jack learns at Oxford, he may never do anything much. He's only going to be a lawyer. So dull!'

'I loathe lawyers,' said Anthony. 'They generally mean unpleasant lawsuits or the reading of Wills. Is your brother intrigued with some girl at the moment?'

'I'm not sure. I rather believe there's someone up at Oxford.'

'Is he attractive?'

'*I* think he's good-looking,' said Joan.

'Then it's a certainty he's got a girlfriend somewhere, If I know anything about human nature.'

'I think you know an awful lot.'

'Too much,' he said wearily.

'I wish I knew more.'

'I shall have to teach you.' He put the glass down and started to play with her hair again. 'And so the Little Fox has no hound in pursuit?'

'No.'

'What a waste of a sweet Little Fox! I think it's my duty to say 'Tally Ho!' and get this hunt going.'

She did not know what to answer to that, so she gave her excited little laugh. Anthony looked down at her face and found it both pure and provocative. He knew that she was quite inexperienced and that he ought to leave her alone. On the other hand, he toyed with the idea of constituting himself her teacher.

He would teach her the art of living. It was what she asked for. What she wanted. She was obviously an emotional, pliable young creature, and if he did not teach her, somebody else would. It would be a pity if it should be one of these crude boys. She would so much more enjoy her first love-affair with a man of sophistication.

'When am I going to see you again, Little Fox?'

'I don't know.'

'What are you doing?'

'Nothing, really,' she said, rather ashamed of the fact.

'Are you always in town?'

'Except at the end of July and August, when we go for a holiday. We always have one every year — the whole family — at some seaside place.'

'It sounds too deadly, my dear.'

'It is,' said Joan, and was a little ashamed of having said so when she thought about her mother's goodness and what nice holidays they had had in the past.

'Preserve me,' said Anthony, 'from communal enjoyment on a beach, where one gets both bored and blistered.'

'I know,' said Joan, and sighed.

'You should come with me for that week of Mediterranean madness instead.'

'Oh, don't!'

'Think!' he continued, enjoying her reaction, 'of an hotel looking over a sea so blue that it makes your eyes ache. Think of golden days, running up into the mountains in my car, stopping at the little inns for superlative meals — the best food and wines in France. Think of the silver nights. Those great big stars. The perfume of the flowers — a million carnations. And I should make marvellous dresses for you to wear. I should be so proud of walking with you through the Casino. And then we'd go back in the car to our hotel. We'd have lovely big rooms with balconies opening out to the sea. The moonlight is unearthly there, and the glamour — intoxicating!'

'Please don't go on,' said Joan, 'when you know I've got to do my three weeks shrimping in England.'

He set down his empty glass and took her hand.

'But supposing I picked you up and put you in a 'plane and flew you to Paris and then to the south — you wouldn't be able to go shrimping in the bosom of your family.'

She caught her breath and laughed.

'You know I couldn't.'

'*I* could.'

'Then *I* couldn't.'

'Why?'

She hesitated. She was not very good at this sort of conversation. And she was much too inexperienced to deal with an emotional situation with the ease and humour that she knew it called for . . . if it was not serious. She never for a moment supposed that Anthony Downe was being serious in his suggestion that she should go to the south of France with him. Yet he was pressing the subject. She said:

'One can't just go off on trips like that — can one?'

'I repeat — *I* could.'

Flushed and uneasy, she looked up at him.

'With any woman, do you mean?'

'Not anyone, just *the* one.'

'You mean your wife?'

'My wife for a week. By the way, that sounds rather like a twopenny novelette,' he said, laughing.

'Oh, I see,' said Joan, crimson. 'Well, I wouldn't be anybody's wife for a week.'

He liked the determined way in which she said that. It amused him highly to carry on the discussion.

'Ah-ha! Now I'm being reproved for my laxity of morals.'

That worried her. She didn't want Anthony to think she was criticizing him or that she was a prude. But there were limits . . . surely! At Lausanne there'd been a girl whose sister had gone away with a man for a weekend and there'd been a frightful scandal

186

about it. It had broken her mother's heart. Joan could well imagine how heartbroken her own mother would be if she calmly walked off to the south of France with Anthony Downe.

'Just for pure interest — I'm not sure that *pure* isn't the wrong word — I'd like to ask you on what grounds you would refuse to come with me,' said Anthony. 'That is, if you liked me sufficiently to spend a week with me.'

'On lots of grounds.'

'Mainly moral ones?'

'In a way, yes,' she confessed. 'But even if I personally wanted to do a thing like that, I couldn't because of my mother and father.'

'That's what I'm getting at,' he said. 'It isn't really you. It's the family. You abide by the traditions and principles of the past generation. All quite wrong, Little Fox — if you don't mind my saying so. Although your maiden aunts would tell you it's all quite right.'

Joan, floundering a bit, sought to carry on the debate with sincerity, although at the back of her mind she dreaded that this marvellous and exciting man, who attracted her so vitally, should find her a bore and dismiss her from his life after tonight. It would be too awful if she could never see Anthony Downe again.

'You can really maintain that it's right for two people who aren't married to go away together!' she said.

'My dear child, it's all a question of what one considers right and wrong. My morals might not agree with your mother's. They certainly wouldn't! Only I follow the dictates of my own conscience and you abide by the conscience of those who are still in authority over you.'

'But they are right,' persisted Joan.

'Only according to standardized convention. Personally, I do not think that a marriage licence necessarily justifies two people living together. If they are unhappily married, I think that the legal tie is the invention of the devil. It is far more angelic for two people who really love each other to live in real happiness, but without the sanction of Church or registrar.'

'Why must a legal union necessarily be unhappy?'

'I don't say it is, always. But you'll admit that nine out of ten marriages are mistakes.'

'I suppose so,' said Joan slowly.

'Shouldn't marriage be the most divine and absolute union of two people's minds and bodies?'

'Yes.'

'How often is it the case? Yet some of my happiest friends are what the world calls 'living in sin'.'

'But,' said Joan, 'living in sin doesn't necessarily constitute happiness.'

'I agree,' said Anthony, thinking of Veronica. 'But if illicit lovers find they don't hit it off, they can at least part easily. A married couple have to go through limitless trouble and expense in order to get a divorce. My own parents were miserably unhappy and couldn't get divorced because my mother was a Roman Catholic and her Church wouldn't allow it. So they lived in hell, and as a small boy my first memories were of them shouting at each other and of my mother crying in the night.'

'How ghastly!'

'That's an extreme case. But how many married people do you know who, even though not actively miserable, are just bored and dissatisfied. What about your own parents?'

For the first time in her life, Joan considered this aspect of her parents. It puzzled and disturbed her. It had never entered her head before to wonder whether or not her mother and father were happily married. They seemed quite peaceful. They didn't have ghastly rows or anything and she had never heard her mother 'crying in the night'. At the same time, she couldn't truthfully say that they were a very well-matched pair. Dear old Pop was awfully kind and nice, but he must be a bore to live with. Mummy was much more go-ahead and amusing when she wanted to be. And she must have been awfully pretty. She still was. What *had* she got out of her marriage? Not much, surely. But try as she would, Joan could not begin to imagine any ecstasies between her parents. In fact, it seemed rather indecent to try to do so.

'Well, Little Fox, out with it,' said Anthony Downe.

'I don't really know,' she said slowly. 'I suppose my parents are as happy as people of that age should be. They're both over forty.'

'Listen to the infant! My good child, I'm going to be forty in less than nine years. Don't tell me that in nine years' time I shall be finished, or that when I'm forty I can no longer expect to be wildly happy with any woman. There are plenty of women, too, of forty and over who fall in love and have mad affairs. Some say that neither a woman nor a man begins to know what really intense feeling is until they've passed their youth. Don't tell me that you, yourself, are going to say goodbye to passion and happiness once you're your mother's age. Why shouldn't you be just as vital then as you are now?'

Joan made no reply. She sat helplessly staring at him. She supposed he was right and it was all rather awful. Forty seemed so dreadfully old to her. She really could not connect her mother and father with the sort of emotions that Anthony was discussing.

'Don't let it worry you. I was merely talking. Let's go back to the other point. As to whether you'd refuse to go abroad with me because of your own principles or because of your family.'

'My own, I think,' she said in a low voice.

'I admire you for that. But I don't altogether believe you. I think you'd turn down the invitation mainly because of all the sorrow you'd bring on the 'old folks at home'. Isn't that it?'

'I don't see that it really matters.'

'It might. It might, if I said 'Little

Fox, I want you to come away with me'.'

She felt at once thrilled and miserable. She really could not argue with Anthony. She was sure that he was not serious and yet — one awful truth struck her — if he did put that question to her seriously, in her heart she knew that, against her principles, *she would want to go*. That seemed horribly wrong and confusing.

She took refuge in looking at her wrist-watch.

'I think I must go home.'

'The Little Fox is frightened?'

'Not in the least,' she said indignantly.

He slid off the arm of her chair and stood up.

'I am. Of you and your youth and your innocence.'

She stood up, too, her fingers locked nervously behind her back. Like a silly schoolgirl, she thought, furious not to be able to meet Anthony Downe on his own ground. But he just bewildered her and enthralled her at the same time.

He took both her hands and drew her closer to him. She was exciting him by that suggestion of aloofness in her, coupled with the unconscious provocation of the young, slender body in the white dress, and the sweet, very young mouth.

'You're an enchanting child,' he murmured.

Then he caught her close and kissed her.

BOOK FIVE

1

Clare Tardy sat in her drawing-room on a fine June evening, darning a pair of her husband's socks. She reflected that it was very pleasant to have Joan at home for once. She had been out such a lot lately. Guy was at home tonight, too, but after dinner he had gone into his consulting-room to try out a new record. They could hear the faint strains of a grand theme rising from below.

Joan lolled in a chair opposite her mother, turning over the pages of an old *Vogue*.

It was quiet and peaceful in the room. The curtains were not yet drawn. It was still light. It had been a fine, warm day. Clare was pleasantly tired, having done a morning's shopping, and been to an 'At Home' given by the wife of a well-known surgeon to whom Guy

197

took his patients for particular diagnoses. Quite a grand affair, and Clare was sociable enough to like a gathering of people, especially when she knew quite a number of them. She still wore the new blue and white spring suit which she had bought for the occasion. It would have to last her for the rest of the summer! It had a tailored silk blouse with a little blue and white bow at the throat. She looked young and slim in it. Joan had told her at dinner that it suited her. From Joan, that was praise indeed. Although Clare modestly declared that her 'slimness' was due to a new and very satisfactory elastic belt.

There was no getting away from the fact that Clare was worried about her elder daughter. Jack had gone back to Oxford and Mogs to school. But although Joan was the only one left at home, her mother hardly ever saw her.

Since that night when she had gone to dinner with her new friends, Joan had led a hectic life. When Clare drew Guy's attention to the fact, he said that it was bad for the girl's health to be out so much and so late. Night after night, Joan went to theatres, parties or dances. Clare had to admit that it suited her in a way. She seemed to have blossomed out these last few weeks. She was never morose or discontented now. Always brimming over with excitement. On the other hand, she was still guarded in what she said. She talked about her good times, but always, the mother felt, with discretion. She was sure, too, that Joan was losing weight; growing too thin and big-eyed. It would only have started a scene had Clare tried to make her eat more or go to bed earlier. Once or twice she had considered asking Guy to speak to her. Then she had thought better of it. No use treating Joan as though she were still the same age as Mogs. She could only give her good advice and leave it at that. Joan had got to make her own life and gain her own experience. Clare did not want to interfere. But she yearned for her daughter's confidence.

Joan put down her *Vogue* and stood up.

'I think I'll go out for a walk, Mum.'

'Oh!' said Clare disappointed. 'I hoped we were going to have a nice little evening together.'

'I'm feeling restless,' said Joan.

'You want a good night's sleep. You weren't in bed last night till the early hours. *Do* go to bed early tonight, darling.'

'I will,' said Joan.

Clare looked at her. Really, she was absurdly thin, especially in that dinner dress. And she was not at all the old Joan. This was a chic young lady — like a fashionable figure out of that *Vogue* which she had been reading. The long black skirt made her hips look very narrow. The smart little flowered coat had square, exaggerated shoulders, and was drawn by a belt tightly in at the waist. It was a dress by Anthony Downe. Nearly all Joan's old clothes had been scrapped. Everything she wore now bore that little ivory satin label with the scarlet name stamped upon it: *Anthony Downe*.

Joan said that the Downes were making her things at half the usual price because she had become a friend. And as she no longer demanded advances on her allowance, Clare saw no reason to object.

'Don't go out this evening,' Clare coaxed. 'Stay with me. I've had such an amusing letter from Moggie; I want to read it to you.'

Joan took a cigarette from a box on the table by the fireplace and lit it. She wondered if her mother realized how pale she was under her rouge. Indeed, if her mother realized that she was using rouge these days. It was so natural and well put on. Agatha had taught her the art of make-up, just as Tony had taught her about clothes.

'Read me Mogs' letter, darling,' she said to her mother mechanically.

But she only half heard her young sister's long effusion, full of the usual remarks about her beloved Miss

Walters, boasting about her victories on the tennis court, asking for something to be sent. There was never a letter from Mogs in which there wasn't a request for something she 'must have *at once*'.

Joan was thinking about Tony. She marvelled how completely one could change in a few weeks. Was it only six weeks ago since she had gone back with him to his flat after the new revue, and he had taken her in his arms? He had been marvellous.

If she had fallen in love with him before that experienced kiss which he had laid upon her lips, she had been ten times more in love after it. She admired him, too, because of his control. He might so easily have taken advantage of the emotions which he knew he roused in her. Today, she was a little ashamed of those young, crude emotions. Thank God, he had taught her to be subtle and restrained. But he had very wisely sent her home.

And there had been other nights

when he had sent her home. Yet he was in love with her. He said so. There was nothing he hadn't said, except that he wanted to marry her. That was the one burning anxiety in Joan Tardy's heart.

He was grand to her in every way. Gave her lovely presents. Made her clothes at a nominal price and only accepted payment because she insisted. Took her to exciting parties such as she had never dreamed about. Turned the unsophisticated schoolgirl into a woman of the world. At least, that was how she looked upon herself these days. But marriage, Anthony never mentioned. The trip to the south of France, however, he never ceased to allude to, always hinting that one day they would take it. That was what preyed on her mind when she was away from him.

For while she clung to the old shibboleths, she half-despised herself for being a coward. She was terrified of the ultimate end to this breathless episode. She knew that he was not the man to settle down to domestic bliss. Knew, too, that he would not always be patient and controlled. The day would come when he would not want to send her home. And then! Then for the catastrophe, Joan continually told herself.

There were times when she wanted to pour out her troubles to her mother. There were times when it was almost too much for her, and she half-wished that she could go back to being that simple sort of girl who had left Lausanne. But she refrained from enlightening Clare. Poor darling! She would never in a thousand years understand Anthony, or his kind. She would just forbid her to see Anthony again and then there'd be unceasing rows and trouble. No, she had got to go through this thing alone.

Of course, she might have told Jack. Only Jack was modern and broadminded about other men's sisters, but might not be so about his own. Because she was only eighteen, he would want to tell their mother. Much better not to put him in a difficult position.

One curious thing that had evolved from this tempestuous affair with Anthony, reflected Joan, was her new friendship with Christopher Fenlick. The young artist often came round here in the evenings, now. She had even started posing for a 'head and shoulders' in his studio. She wished to give a sketch of herself to Tony. And, incidentally, she had found virtues in Chris which she had never noticed before. Something apart from his quiet charm. Common sense. Knowledge of the world. (He seemed years older to her than Jack.) And Understanding.

During one of his sittings, she had actually hinted that she was going through an awful strain because of some man who didn't believe in marriage. Chris had not seemed shocked or surprised. Neither had he started to lecture her. He had just been awfully nice and sympathetic. He had agreed that there were people in the world who abided by their own morals and shut out convention. People who really preferred their pleasures to be illegal. He neither condemned nor condoned such an attitude. He said it was a matter of personal opinion and that on all occasions one should be true to oneself. The main piece of advice which he gave her was never for a moment to allow her real self or feelings to be clouded by infatuation. Nor should she, he said, let anybody exercise over her an influence which would eventually create that cloud.

His advice had given her a lot to think about. For she knew that she was, for the moment, entirely influenced by Anthony. Not only physically but mentally. She wanted desperately to belong to him altogether. But if she gave way, then she would be doing what Chris warned her against. She would be untrue to her real self. For, look at it how she might, she did not honestly believe that life could be lived successfully without good sound morals. Neither could she fail to see that

Anthony's outlook was purely egotistical.

Still, she could not bear the thought of there being no Tony in her life. That was the worst of it. Every day, at some time or other, for the last six weeks she had seen him, or they spoke over the telephone. The only thing he did not do was to write. He never wrote letters.

Her mother's voice penetrated her turbulent thoughts. Still reading from Mog's epistle.

'I'm simply dying for the hols. The place you've chosen sounds lovely, Mum . . . '

As this penetrated Joan's imagination, she gave a little grimace. That holiday at Kymer Cove! How she dreaded it! Three whole weeks away from London and Tony. And somehow she felt ashamed of the holiday to which he alluded as the 'Beach and Blister'. He didn't want her to go. He said he was so afraid of 'some other hound getting on to the scent of his Little Fox'. Well, that was a needless fear. She could not imagine anybody taking his place for an instant. But she did not want to leave him or London.

Mogs was possibly the only one who did look forward to Kymer Cove. Jack didn't. She was in Jack's confidence at the moment. He had told her about the girl in Oxford. He had run short of money, and not wanting to ask Father or Mother, had borrowed from her. He had got round her by appealing to her romantic side. In a letter which she had received at the beginning of the week, he had mentioned somebody called Amanda, who, he said, was 'the most heavenly person'. He wanted to buy her a birthday present. Joan had sent a pound. She could sympathize with Jack if he were in love. With the money, she wrote a note, telling him that she was thrilled about his girlfriend and wanted to meet her when he came down again.

Tonight, Joan felt very grown-up and experienced and just a little cynical as she looked at her mother. Darling Mother, sitting there darning Daddy's socks so peacefully! What did she know of her children? Or the madness and ecstasy and misery of passionate love? She could never have loved poor old Pop that way. She was lucky to have been spared all the raptures and the agonies.

'When I'm forty I shall be finished,' Joan told herself dramatically.

Then uneasily, she remembered Tony telling her that some women didn't begin to live until they were forty.

'There, darling,' said Clare, folding Mogs' letter. 'And do remind me to send off that new grip Moggie wants for her racquet-handle. Perhaps you would go to Lillywhites tomorrow and get her one.'

'Okay,' said Joan.

'Are you looking forward to Kymer Cove?' asked Clare brightly.

Joan nodded without answering.

'I think it's a pity we don't ask Chris to go down with us. He has no home and he's working very hard. Shall we ask him if he'd like to go with us?'

'I don't mind,' said Joan.

But she was thinking:

'This is the first day Tony hasn't rung me or seen me. I can't go to bed until I've spoken to him. I *can't*'

Then the telephone rang. The colour sprang to Joan's cheeks.

'Your father's in the consulting-room,' said Clare. 'He'll answer it.'

'It may be for me.'

'Well, listen-in, darling, and find out.'

Joan tore into her mother's bedroom. Her hand shook as she put the receiver to her ear. It might be Tony. It *must* be. Her heart sank as she heard a brisk, dry voice saying:

'The pulse is quite good, but I don't know that it wouldn't be wise to let Nurse give another hypodermic . . . '

Joan put down the telephone.

'Oh, damn! *Damn!*' she said, between her teeth.

She waited a moment, smoking a cigarette, giving her father time to finish his conversation, then dialled the number of Anthony's flat. She was answered by the flat-valet who happened to be there.

'No, madam, Mr. Downe is not in . . . Yes, madam, he'll be back, because he isn't changed, and he sent a message that he was at a show which would keep him until nine and that then he must come back to dress for a late party.'

Joan's heart was beating fast.

'You think he'll be there at any moment?'

'I should think so, madam. It's about nine now.'

Joan made up her mind to go round to Anthony's flat. She had never done such a thing before without an invitation. Perhaps it wasn't being very tactful. On the other hand, the Downes were such easy-going people, and Tony always said he liked his friends to drop in and out as they wished. And she knew he would want to see his 'Little Fox'. How she adored that name and the way he said it. The way he looked at her. The way he kissed her. Damn, *damn!* If only she wasn't so frightfully in love, it would be easier.

She ran up to her room and changed from her dinner-dress into a black coat and skirt and a smart white satin shirt which Anthony had made for her. With this outfit she wore a black Breton sailor hat on the back of her red-brown head. He liked her in that hat. She made up her face again, and went downstairs to the drawing-room to her mother.

She found it necessary to lie. She hated doing it. Lies and intrigues were not really in her line. She said:

'I must get out for a breath of air, Mum, so I think I'll go round to Chris's studio and ask him if he'd like to come down to Kymer Cove with us.'

'All right, darling,' said Clare, and resigned herself to an evening which meant either staying up here alone with her darning, or sitting beside Guy who would eventually stop playing his gramophone and fall asleep.

2

Joan walked up and down Anthony's white drawing-room. She paused every now and then to look with nervous, restless eyes through the open window. The boxes of geraniums on the roof outside were a brilliant scarlet against the pale blue sky. The chimney-tops looked like sharp, black silhouettes.

She wished that Tony would come. The valet had let her in, assuring her that Mr. Downe would be here any minute. She had waited half an hour already. Every now and again, she made up her mind to run away before he came back. She did not want him to think she was hurling herself at his head. But amongst the many things he had tried to teach her was the equality of the sexes in matters of love. He disapproved of that 'wait until you're asked' attitude

213

of the girls of the past generation.

Joan helped herself to a cocktail. That was another thing he had taught her. 'Don't wait for an invitation to a drink if you see one . . . just take it.'

She walked up to the piano and looked at the loose sheets of music lying on the lid. One was Tony's new dance number, 'Little Fox', for which that awful man, Pony, had written the words. Pony was still Agatha's constant companion. Joan could not pretend that she liked Agatha. She was afraid of her sharp tongue and critical eye and felt that there was something evil about her. Tony, himself, said that his sister was a bad woman but that he liked her and that she had an unfailing eye for clothes.

There came the sound of a key being inserted in the latch. Joan swung round from the window. She stood, flushed and expectant, heart hammering.

With his easy, graceful walk, Anthony came into the room. He looked pale, tired and more languid than usual. He was working hard on a new revue which was being dressed by his firm. The heat and work together did not suit him.

When he saw the slender girl in black waiting for him he paused, astonished. Then he came forward in his slightly theatrical manner, arms outstretched.

'Dar-*ling!* What a divine surprise.'

That set at rest all her fears that he might not be pleased to see her. With a single movement, she swept off her hat and flung herself into his arms.

'Tony!'

He kissed and caressed her, and whispered:

'Sweet Little Fox . . . my Little Fox! What brought you from your lair?'

'I had to see you,' she said in a muffled voice, her head against his shoulder.

'Why, you're trembling, angel. What is it?'

'You haven't 'phoned me all day — I couldn't think what had happened.'

Then he released her, shaking his head.

'My sweet, *don't* be boring! I'm a working man and I haven't had a *moment!* I've had to get out a dozen designs for Ducayne. That show's frightfully important to me, as you know.'

She stood, chilled and reproved.

'Sorry, perhaps I oughtn't to have come.'

'But it's so enchanting to see you, sweet . . . '

He stepped back and gazed at her with a look which was now so familiar . . . the critical professional eye travelling up and down.

'God! I must say that's a well-cut suit, even though one of my tailors made it. It's a divine line.'

She was silent. She didn't care about her suit or his praise of it. She wanted him to tell her that he wasn't bored. He had said: '*Don't be boring.*' She had never heard him say anything so unkind before.

The wisdom and sophistication with which she liked to cloak herself fell away, leaving the still ignorant, gauche schoolgirl. Nervously, she said:

'You're going out somewhere, I expect. I'd better say goodbye.'

He was going out. And with Veronica. That devil of a woman had been making things pretty warm for him lately. Someone had told her that he was running round with a young girl. Veronica had threatened to leave Porteous and drag him into a divorce. That was the last thing he wanted. The scandal didn't matter a fig, but he didn't want to be tied to 'Egypt' for the rest of his life. He had long since come to the conclusion that Mark Antony had been a raving idiot. He did not intend to follow in his footsteps.

But he had got to take Veronica out to supper tonight. There was no getting away from that. He would rather have stayed here with this child who so palpably and rather pathetically adored him. Now that he was making her dress properly and had taught her a few things, she was a damned attractive young woman. At the same time, he was getting a bit tired of playing the rôle of the strong man, resisting temptation. It was a bit of a bore. He did so loathe being bored. Or being made to do anything that was an effort. All the same, he was still feeling what Agatha called 'lecherous' about the Little Fox. And in the circumstances, as the girl was so much in love, he wondered whether it wouldn't be a kindness on his part to withstand temptation no longer.

He made a rapid mental calculation. Nine-thirty. He wasn't meeting Veronica until half-past eleven at Quaglino's. That would give him two hours with Joan.

He gave her his dark, significant smile and touched her hair. She no longer wore it in curls, but as he liked it, parted in the centre, two burnished wings brushed back from her forehead. Most attractive, he considered.

'Listen, angel . . . you're going to sit

down and take a drink and a cigarette while I have my bath and change. Then I'll come back and talk to you.'

Joan felt happy again.

'Do you really want me to?'

'I wouldn't suggest it if I didn't.'

She smiled and sat down.

Anthony poured himself out a drink, drank it, then switched on the radio. Someone was singing with a dance-band:

'*I've tried so not to give in,*
I said to myself this affair never
will go so well . . .'

Anthony switched it off.

'I'm sick of the tune, but I like the words.'

She looked up at him.

'So do I.'

Then he had one of those moments when passion leaped unaware and made him utterly ruthless.

He put his hands on the arm of the chair, leaning right over Joan. He quoted softly:

'Don't you know, little fool, you
never can win.
Use your mentality,
Wake up to reality . . . '

She gave a little gasp. Her throat felt
constricted. Her whole body burned.
She had never seen that look . . . quite
that look . . . in Anthony's eyes before.
Never noticed how hard and compelling his mouth could be.

He was pulling her up into his arms.

'You know, Little Fox, you never can
win . . . you'd better wake up to that
now . . . tonight. You *have* got me under
your skin, haven't you, darling? Haven't
you?'

'Yes, but — '

'No 'buts' tonight, my sweet. I think
we've been very good quite long
enough.'

So it had come. The moment she
had anticipated and dreaded. Anthony
wasn't going to 'be good' any longer.
And he wasn't going to let her remain
so, either. This was going to be the big

test. The struggle between the Joan who was herself, the Joan who belonged to him, and that Joan who still belonged to her family.

If only he wouldn't kiss her like that! Touch her like that! That cruel, irresistible mouth of his travelled from her lips to her throat; those slender, clever fingers slid under the satin of her shirt, over her shoulders, down her back . . .

She wanted, more than she had ever wanted anything in this life, to abandon herself completely to this man.

'Little Fox,' Anthony urged her, 'you're going to give in, aren't you? And you're not going down to Cornwall with the family next month. You're coming to France with me.'

Somehow, it was the mention of that holiday in Cornwall which saved Joan from herself and from him. That awful family holiday which they jeered at, sneered at, dreaded, yet in their heart of hearts enjoyed and accepted because it was part of the pattern of their communal existence. A pattern which no single one of them had the right to destroy. Even if she had a right to destroy herself, she could not hurt them as badly as it would hurt if she gave way to Anthony Downe tonight, then went away with him. Having done the one thing, the other would follow.

'Darling,' said Anthony sharply. 'What's the matter? Why don't you kiss me?'

She put her hands on his shoulders and looked at him. Her face was colourless except for the rouge on her cheek-bones. She said, in a voice that had no life in it:

'I can't, Tony. I *can't*.'

'But — if you love me?'

'It isn't fair of you!'

'My sweet, surely we're not striking a bargain or asking what is fair or unfair of each other? If we love, it is right and natural to give way to it.'

Agonized, Joan continued to look up at him.

'I know you feel that way, Tony. Perhaps I do, too. But you've got nobody to say what you should or shouldn't do, and I have — the family.'

Passion died in Anthony Downe. It left him without a vestige of feeling for her, even of pity. If he had any pity it was for himself because he had been thwarted, and was annoyed that this slip of a girl should deny him what Veronica and a good many other women in his life had begged for on bended knees. He said violently:

'Oh, to hell with your family. I'm sick to death of the mention of them. I'm concerned with you, not your mother and father and sister and brother. It's really too boring. And I'm much too tired to argue with you. But since you obviously prefer your family to me — we'd better call it a day.'

Her gaze never left his face. She could not speak for a moment. She felt cold and frightened. She knew that she had lost him. That in itself was catastrophic. She was frightened of what lay before her. Of how she would suffer without him. Then she said:

'Oh, Anthony — I'm so sorry. But you've got your point of view, and I must have mine.'

He picked up her hat and handed it to her.

'You're quite entitled to it, my dear. And I'm a cad, but I'm not apologizing for it. You run along and find some hero who plays cricket and football and wears the old school tie as it should be worn. I haven't designed one for myself yet. If I do, I'll ring you up.'

It struck her that he was being so beastly that he spoiled even the memory of every charming and tender thing he had ever said.

Tears came into her eyes, stinging and bitter. She seized her hat, gloves and bag, and without another look at him, turned and ran from the room.

For a moment he stood with his hands in his pockets, glowering at the floor. Then he walked up to the piano, picked up the sheet of manuscript marked 'Little Fox', and yawned.

It was much too much of an effort

trying to get over a young girl's complexes about her family. He'd give inviolate youth a miss in the future. He'd better tear up this number, too. But no, the music was good. He'd make Pony write some more words for it. To hell with that girl and with Veronica Porteous, and all women! Why couldn't they leave a man alone? He felt too utterly shattered.

Well, the 'fox hunt' had been quite amusing while it lasted. But the fox had got away. That had been rather amusing, all that part of it. He grinned suddenly at the memory of what he had said about the old school tie. He must tell Agatha . . .

He began in his mind to design a tie for himself. Yes, he would have one made and send it to Joan with an appropriate message.

3

'Jackie darling, *must* you go away with your family for three whole weeks?' Amanda Deering asked in her most discontented tone.

She was sitting under a tree, smoking and watching Jack clear up the remains of a picnic supper which they had taken outside Oxford. It was a perfect June evening.

Jack Tardy shook some beer drops out of a mug, grimaced as he wiped the unattractive remains of food from a papier-mâché plate, and thought how loathsome everything looked at the end of a picnic, whereas at the beginning it was all so tempting. He toyed with the idea of remarking to Amanda with some drama, that a picnic was symbolic of many things in life. Not so good afterwards as before. Then he decided that this might be taken as an insult by his girlfriend, so he refrained. He answered her good-humouredly.

'You know I've got to go, my sweet.'

'It's such a long time for me to be without you.'

'I'd take you if I could, darling.'

Amanda hunched her shoulders sulkily and looked across the green meadow where a solitary, shaggy horse was grazing patiently regularly shaking his head and whisking his tail against the onslaught of a cloud of flies. She felt no pity for the horse. If anything, her sympathy was with the flies. Just as they imagined they were reaching a nice portion of that rich brown neck, they were frightened off, thwarted. She felt thwarted. She liked to get her own way in life and make Jack do everything she wanted him to do. It annoyed her because he was taking this holiday with his family instead of with her.

'Where are you going?' she asked gloomily.

'Kymer Cove. My mother's taken rooms at the Headland Hotel. I believe it's quite a decent place, with some surf-bathing. I shall play golf. I'm getting rather keen on it. And there's quite a good little course at Kymer, which is a blessing.'

Amanda wrinkled her nose, then proceeded to powder it. She felt that make-up was as necessary here, out in the country, as in her dance-room.

'It sounds frightful to me, and for heaven's sake don't start becoming one of these wretched golfing maniacs.'

'Why 'maniacs'?'

'Well, people who take up golf can never do it reasonably. They have to talk about it all day and spend every available instant on the links. I would never have believed you could do anything so boring.'

'It doesn't happen to bore me,' said Jack, and finished putting the last bits and pieces into the picnic case, shut it, then lay down on his back. He folded his arms behind his head and looked up at the sky. It was a pure and beautiful sky of translucent blue. The evening star shone with unusual brilliance. There was not a breath of wind to stir the greeny-brown leaves of the oak under which Amanda was sitting.

Jack felt suddenly tired. He was working hard at the moment, facing an important 'exam'. The weather had been hot. He felt he could do with those few weeks' holiday by the sea, even though spent apart from Amanda.

And for the first time since his association with her, he wished that Amanda were just a bit more peaceful. She was such a stormy petrel, always wanting to argue (if they weren't making love) or demanding something which she couldn't have, or grumbling at something which she had got. Madly in love though he was, he regretted these traits in her character.

Here they were, in the country on a heavenly June night, having had a grand meal — lobster-salad, cheese, lager beer. Gosh! They ought to be content. He would have liked Amanda to sit beside him and stroke his hair and

229

listen while he read her extracts from his book of poems by Housman. He was mad about Housman at the moment and wanted to read 'The Shropshire Lad' to Amanda. But one couldn't read poems to a girl who was in a grousing mood.

'I enjoyed that evening we had in London during your last vacation,' she said with a sigh. 'When are we going to have another, Jackie?'

'Next vacation, I suppose.'

'When do you go on this wretched holiday?'

'Not till the end of July.'

'Then couldn't we go away somewhere together at the end of this month?'

Jack scowled and shut his eyes. The old argument was coming up. She knew perfectly well he couldn't take her away without there being a scandal. Why couldn't she be patient and wait until he could marry her. He was on the verge of saying something caustic, then turned his gaze to her and softened.

She looked so very pretty sitting there against the tree. She wore a sleeveless white linen dress with a blue belt around her small waist. From beneath the skirt, her legs emerged bare of stockings, sunbrowned and seductive. She had exquisite feet. They looked marvellous in those toe-less blue sandals, revealing the scarlet varnished nails.

Her head was sleek and of an almost platinum fairness in the evening light, against the dark trunk of the tree. She looked very young tonight. The white linen dress was stretched tightly across her small breasts. And suddenly Jack was excited, rolled over, caught at her hand and pressed it hard. After all, it was a very wonderful thing to know that this lovely girl was his.

'Don't let's argue, Beautiful. Let's just be happy. It will soon be time for me to get back.'

She pouted.

'Honestly, Jack, you seem much more

content to wait for me than I am to wait for you.'

'That couldn't be true. I adore you.'

'Well — you know what I feel about you,' she said, and put some sincerity into her voice.

She was always physically attracted by Jack. He looked his best dressed like this in his old grey flannels, coatless, a light blue shirt with short sleeves showing his brown, muscular arms. His neck was brown and strong. His hair miraculously black. Handsome as a young Apollo. And in his more passionate moments, her abject slave. She liked to exercise her powers over him and get him to the pitch where he was entirely submissive. He was an exciting lover. Not like that dull codfish of a husband of hers, who was so tied up with inhibitions and repressions that he had been embarrassed by the sight of her without her clothes on, and turned out the light as a prelude to love-making.

She had a sudden warm feeling about

Jack. The money didn't matter. Nothing mattered so long as she could feel that she belonged to him. She was so terrified that he would find out something which would alter his regard for her.

She slid toward him and lay with him on the grass, her arms twisting around his neck. A slave-bangle which she wore with a variety of little charms attached to it jingled as she made the movement. She put her lips against his neck.

'Jackie boy!'

His hands caressed her and he held her lips in a long kiss. Then he said:

'You do make me crazy about you. You're the most exciting, lovely person to hold like this. God, Amanda, I don't want to go away from you. You know it.'

'Do you really want me to be happy?'

He smoothed the silky curls back from her warm neck. In this half-light, none of the lines which aged her face in the daytime were visible. She might have been a young girl, lying there in his arms.

'You've been so damned good to me, Amanda. Of course I want you to be happy. And I'd do anything in my power.'

'Then marry me, Jack. If I knew I was your wife it would make all the difference in the world to me.'

'Now, Amanda — '

'I don't mean introduce me to your family. Just marry me and let's go on as we are. Then later, when you've got into a certain position in your uncle's office, you can say that I'm your wife.'

That gave Jack Tardy much food for thought, but it was food he could not digest in an instant. He tried to sit up, but she held him down, straining her slight body against his.

'No, listen, darling, *darling* Jackie. Don't say 'no'. It can't do you any harm — we could be married by special licence at the Register Office. I'd pay for the licence. I've got some savings from the business. I'd do anything, *anything* to feel that I was really yours and that nothing could ever separate us again. Don't you feel like that about me, Jackie? You've always said you wanted to marry me. Then why not now? Why not?'

He relaxed under the pressure of her hands and lay silent, his face crinkled with perplexity. Of course he was going to marry her one day. She was quite right. There was no real reason why they should not have a secret marriage. Only it would upset his mother frightfully when she knew — and his father. Besides which, Uncle Arthur was a difficult man. But he need not produce his wife until he had made some progress in his uncle's office. Then he could bring Amanda forward, and surely the family would not object. She would soon win them round with her charm and beauty.

Amanda went on pleading, punctuating the words with those little butterfly kisses, all over his face, which she knew he could never withstand.

'I love you so much, darling. I *must* feel that you're mine and that I am yours. You say you're jealous of every man who dances with me. You're always afraid I'm going to run off with someone else. But if I was your wife — you'd feel happier about me, wouldn't you?'

'Yes, of course.'

'Just think,' she whispered against his ear, 'if Amanda was Jackie's wife.'

She was being Delilah with a vengeance. He felt his strength slipping from him. She was a witch and he wanted her madly. As her words began to permeate, he thought what a thrill it would be to marry her secretly. She was right. He would not be jealous if he knew she was his wife. And he was, fiendishly so, now when he was away from Oxford, picturing all the other men who were after her — men who thought they had as much right as he had, to take her out.

'Say 'yes' to me, darling,' Amanda whispered.

'It's a frightfully serious thing, darling,' he whispered back, stroking her hair. 'And I must just think it over. I'll think tonight and tell you in the morning.'

She felt maddened, but she could not press the point further without irritating him.

He began to make love to her more passionately.

'You're such a temptation, Amanda. God! I think I'll have to marry you and be damned to everything else.'

Her heart leaped. She smoothed a black lock of hair from his brown boy's face.

'Jackie darling, how *marvellous!*'

Half an hour later, it was quite dark. They were no longer under the oak tree, but in the open two-seater car which Jack had borrowed from a friend. He sat at the wheel, feeling extraordinarily happy. He had never felt happier about Amanda. She had never been more heavenly than in his arms just now, under the stars. He had reached the conclusion that he had no right to let her feel worried about the future, or be for an instant anxious lest he should not put things on a proper basis. He owed it to her to marry her. And marry her he would, secretly, as she suggested. The future must take care of itself.

Amanda sat beside him, combing her curls, twining every silvery ringlet round her finger. She was very pleased with herself. Jack threw away his cigarette and looked at the blue linen bag which was lying on her lap. The light in the dashboard showed up the contents. Cigarette-case, holder, powder-puff in a blue chiffon handkerchief, lipstick and mirror. Everything a little dirty and powdery. And a letter. It was the letter upon which Jack focused his attention, for the address was written on the envelope in a man's small handwriting. He said:

'Who's been writing my girl love-letters?'

He had expected a laughing reply, instead of which Amanda, temporarily startled by something which he did not understand, shoved the letter farther down into her bag and snapped the clasp.

'Nobody.'

It was the start which she gave and the manner in which she shut that bag which put a suspicion into Jack's mind. He was not by nature an inquisitive or suspicious man. But this girl was his and he was frankly jealous of her. Immediately, he took it for granted that what he had just said in jest was the truth. That was a love-letter.

Peace and happiness fell away from him.

'Who's that letter from, darling?'

She gave a nervous little giggle.

'Don't be such a busybody.'

'Well, who is it from?' (No 'darling' this time.)

'A friend.'

'Someone I know?'

'Really, Jack, I don't see why I should be cross-examined about my correspondence.'

'I thought you liked me to be jealous about you.'

'Yes, but I don't expect you to be unnecessarily so.'

A devil entered Jack. When he wanted to be obstinate he was a mule. He wished to see that letter and find out whether Amanda had another lover. If so, he wasn't going to stand for it. Not for a single minute. He had always respected her. Never for an instant criticized her in his mind because she had been generous to him. He fully appreciated her generosity. But he had taken it for granted that she was not equally generous to other men. He would not have her receiving letters which he could not read. With a swift gesture which she did not anticipate, his hand shot out and lifted the bag off her lap. At once she tried to grab it back.

'Jack, how *dare* you!'

He put it behind his back. His young face was set and hard as he looked down at her. Her eyes were afraid — and furiously angry.

'You don't want me to read that letter!'

'I don't see why you should read it.'

'Has a wife any secrets from her husband?'

'I'm not — ' she began, then stopped, biting her lips, enraged.

'You're not my wife, you were just going to say,' he went on with sarcasm. 'On the other hand, you've taken a great deal of trouble tonight to persuade me to marry you at once. Also, I've considered you in the light of a wife ever since our affair began. I have a right to see that letter, and I intend to — if only because you don't want me to see it.'

'You'd better give it back.'

'When I've read it,' he said coolly.

'I don't advise you to.'

'Oh — then there *is* something in it you don't want me to see?'

'Can't I have my own private business? As a matter of fact, the letter is about a secret of Sheila's and there's no reason why you should know that.'

'I don't think I believe you, Amanda.'

She lost her temper and made

another snatch at his hand.

'Give me my bag, you beast.'

He looked at her through narrowed lids. He had never seen her like this before. Her face was convulsed with rage. It made her look old and ugly.

He shook her arm off, opened the bag and pulled out the letter.

She screamed at him hysterically:

'You've no right to read my letters. You've no right. Don't dare. If you do, I'll never speak to you again as long as I live!'

Jack was in a dangerous mood. His blood was up now. He got out of the car in order to elude her snatching fingers, raised the envelope and, by the light of the headlights, read the address.

'*Mrs. James Mackie,*
'*c/o George Deering, Esq.*'

He got no further. *Mrs Mackie.* That was Amanda's married name, which he had only heard once and which he had almost forgotten. He thought of her always as 'Miss Deering'. The postmark was 'Portsmouth'. It struck him in a flash that this letter was from Amanda's husband. The knowledge did not make things any better. He had had no idea that she communicated with her husband. She had never told him that she did. He was incensed by the knowledge that she kept such secrets from him. He heard her shouting at him from inside the car.

'You'll be sorry all your life if you read that letter.'

But the devil that was in Jack would not let him heed her warning. He took the letter from the envelope and began to read. And gradually, all jealousy and suspicion, all feelings of pique or annoyance, fell away from him. Left him cold. Left him amazed. And finally, left him so sick at heart that he could hardly speak.

That letter from James Mackie told him many things that he did not know. It was, in effect a terrible indictment against Amanda. And the most important information it contained was that she had a child. That child, a boy, had been operated on for appendicitis two days ago. Complications set in and the doctors had been afraid that he was dying. James Mackie, much against his will, telegraphed his one-time wife to ask her to go to the hospital because the boy had asked for his mother. And she had not gone. *She had not gone.* That was what struck Jack Tardy as even more frightful than the fact that she had deceived him, and never mentioned her child.

He was fond of children. He could not conceive of any human being being unkind to a child, let alone one who was dying. That was what stood out in his mind at this moment as the most appalling reproach against Amanda. The unforgivable crime. The other things were negligible. Such matters, for instance, as deceiving him about her age. This letter mentioned that the boy would have been ten had he lived. That must make Amanda over thirty. *Eleven years older than himself*, thought Jack, hot and scarlet and trembling.

'*I can forgive you for what you did to me just before our divorce*,' James Mackie ended his letter, '*but never for refusing Jim's wish to see you. You were never fit to be his mother, but as he asked for you, I expected you to come. I loved the boy, but the only consolation I have, now that he is dead, is that that bit in him which was you, is dead also . . .* ' It was signed: '*James Mackie*'.

For a while Jack stood there, the letter crushed in his hand. He felt unable to think straight or speak. The woman in the car was sobbing now. The whole story seemed to unfold itself clearly for Jack. This letter did not appear to be the letter of the utter brute she had always described her husband, but just the tragic outcry of a quiet, ordinary man who had lost his son.

Amanda must have left that son callously when she left James Mackie. Jack knew now that not one word she had told him about the divorce was true.

This, then, was the woman who was his first love, of whom he had thought as a young girl, cruelly treated by life. This was the lover he had held in his arms. This the person whom he had been about to marry.

There leaped into Jack's mind a consciousness of all the shame of it and the escape he had had. But the escape made the thing nonetheless shameful. Yesterday he had taken Amanda to a cinema. Yesterday her son had died. He felt almost as though he had helped to keep her away from the boy's death-bed.

For a moment he stood there, in a state of shock which left him physically sick. Then he pulled himself together and turned to Amanda. He put the letter back into the bag and flung it on her lap.

Without a word he took his place at the wheel and switched on the engine.

As the car started to move forward, Amanda, cowed and frightened, lifted her head. Her face was smeared with running eyelash-black and rouge. He did not notice it. She began:

'Jack — Jack, don't go yet. Wait . . . Let me explain.'

He pressed his foot on the accelerator, turned the car out of the lane on to the main Godstow Road leading back to Oxford, and said:

'Why didn't you go to that boy, when you knew he was dying?'

'Jack — wait — '

'Why didn't you go? he repeated inexorably.

'Please — '

'That's the only answer I want from you.' She began to sob again.

'You're terribly hard and cruel. You won't even let me explain.'

'I don't see what there is to explain. You went to the cinema with me. You should have gone down to Portsmouth.'

'I — I didn't see the use of going. I hadn't seen Jim for so long. It might have upset him to see me. I didn't think he'd die.'

'Don't be fantastic. You were told he was dying. You were asked to go, and you should have gone. Good God! You're worse than the lowest woman alive. There are common prostitutes who would have more feeling for their own children.'

'Oh!' she moaned.

'Well, he's dead. And I should think you'll have that on your conscience as long as you live.'

She made no answer. She cried helplessly, raging secretly and impotently. She could have killed James for writing that letter, and she would never forgive herself for keeping it in her bag. But she had never dreamed this would happen.

She knew she had lost Jack Tardy. She did not even waste her time pleading with him. Neither had she any adequate answer when he said:

'And you would have married me without telling me about your son, or letting me know your age. For a first-class baby-snatcher, you should exhibit a little more love of children.'

That made her curl up. He did not speak again until they reached her home in the Woodstock Road. He drew up at the house, got out, opened the door for her politely and said in a frozen voice:

'You won't, of course, expect our marriage to take place. As I am very distressed that you went to the pictures with me yesterday instead of going down to the hospital, I'd like you to take this . . . '

He pulled a ten-shilling note from his pocket. It was half the money which Joan had sent him, and which he had meant to spend on Amanda's birthday present.

'Please buy some flowers . . . to be sent to the child's funeral.'

Her fingers closed automatically over the note. She no longer sobbed. Sullen and silent, she stood before him, and he wondered with an intolerable sickness of soul how he had ever loved her.

He added:

'If you spend the money on yourself instead of the flowers, I shan't know. Goodbye.'

He got back into his car and drove away.

When he got home, he was glad to find that the man with whom he shared rooms was already in bed and asleep. He did not feel that he could face anybody in the world.

He sat on the edge of his bed and leaned his head in his hands. That awful feeling of nausea hadn't left him yet. He couldn't believe that this thing had happened and that he would never see Amanda again. His one consolation was that he did not want to see her. She was no longer the enchanting and beloved figure of his imagination. She was a heartless, cruel little bitch, who could not be bothered to go to the bedside of her dying son. And nearly, very nearly, he had married her. He might have taken that creature to his mother and said: 'She is my wife.'

It struck him suddenly that old Chris would be glad this thing had ended. Chris had never liked Amanda. Perhaps he had seen through her. But even Chris would be staggered by this piece of news.

He thought:

'Thank God it won't be long before the end of term. The sooner I get out of Oxford, where I needn't run any risk of seeing her, the better. I wish we were going down to Cornwall a bit sooner. The farther away I get, the better . . .'

Then, suddenly, he remembered nothing save that he had once placed all his love and his faith in Amanda.

He turned and flung himself face downwards on his bed. He lay there, his body shaking, his tears drenching the pillow.

BOOK SIX

1

Clare Tardy very rarely had a row with anybody, but when she did it was a good one. She was having a row now with the manageress of the Headland Hotel in Kymer Cove. The Tardys had arrived. Clare had left the family outside on the wide sunporch which faced the sea, and stood alone at the reception-office, hot, breathless and very angry, prepared to battle.

'But I *booked* a front single room months ago. I wrote in May, especially so that there should be no doubt about my getting what I wanted. It was for my son. I won't have him shoved into a back room, just because you have made a mistake. It's gross negligence on your part, and I'm not going to suffer for it.'

The book-keeper at the desk, a timid little woman with a fringe, quailed before her ledger. She had made the mistake. She felt that the wrath of the manageress, Miss Minter, would descend upon her once they were alone. At the moment, however, in order to keep up the reputation of the hotel, Miss Minter was disclaiming any responsibility.

'I'm sure you must be mistaken, Mrs. Tardy. You asked for one double room in the front, one double and one single at the back at lower rates.'

'No,' said Clare firmly. 'One double at the back and one double and one single at the front. I have your letter acknowledging mine.'

She dropped the small suitcase in which she carried her few personal and precious belongings which she would not have muddled with the rest of the family luggage, and from her bag drew out a sheet of the Headland Hotel note-paper.

Then Miss Minter quailed with her book-keeper. Mrs. Tardy was methodical and had kept the confirmatory note. Methodical guests were formidable to

Miss Minter. She took the letter, glanced at it over the rim of her glasses, put on a very disapproving expression and said:

'Really! This is very aggravating. Very annoying indeed!'

'It is,' exclaimed Clare. 'And I'm *not* going to have my son put into a back bedroom.'

'Just one moment, please.'

Miss Minter retired into the office, put down the little, frosted glass window which excluded the private office from the gaze of those in the hotel entrance, and entered into confidence with her secretary.

Clare waited, determined not to give in. She was so thirsty that she half-considered swallowing pride and indignation and ordering a long, iced drink. She was so tired that she could hardly keep her eyes open. Oh, those long hours of motoring from London to Cornwall! It had taken them two days. They had to stop for one night at Exeter. And with all of them cooped up in 'The Tortoise' in the sweltering sun, on busy, dusty roads, there was little pleasure in the journey.

Guy and Jack had taken the wheel alternately. When Guy drove it was so slow that all the children grumbled. When Jack took the wheel, Clare felt nervous because he drove so fast, and Guy spent most of the time telling him to go slower. Mogs was such a nuisance in a car, too. She was nearly always sick once or twice during the journey. Joan was all right as a rule, but this year she was very quiet and depressed. She had been like that for the last few weeks. Clare simply did not know what to make of her, but she guessed that it was something to do with Joan's friends, the Downes. She had suddenly stopped seeing them. And a little while back, Clare had heard the girl crying her heart out in the early hours of the morning. Many days following, her face had borne traces of weeping. But she had never confided her troubles to her mother, and Clare was left to make wild guesses. Poor little Joan! Clare was so sorry for her. Possibly she had had a love-affair and it had gone wrong. Whatever it was, she kept it to herself.

Clare was thankful that Chris Fenlick was joining them down here in his own car. In three days' time. He couldn't get away before. He and Joan seemed much better friends these days. He was such a dear. He would do Joan good.

Waiting for Miss Minter's decision, Clare looked through the open doors of the hotel at her family, who were standing in a little group. Guy was pointing out a ship on the horizon. Dear Guy! Somehow he looked quite different from the 'doctor' of their Kensington house. Almost a stranger. He always took on a new personality when he went away. He had special clothes to suit the new person that he became. Grey flannels, cricket shirt, a Khaki-coloured linen coat. He had worn that same coat for years when away on his summer holidays. It was part and parcel of his holiday spirit, as were the sun-glasses which were always taken from a drawer in the roll-top desk, and worn unfailingly to protect his rather weak eyes from the glare.

They must be all tired, hot and bad-tempered, Clare thought tenderly. She couldn't blame them. Joan looked terribly pale. Clare hoped the three weeks in the sun and sea air would soon remedy that. And she really must begin to put on weight. She couldn't get much thinner. She looked very young out there in her blue linen coat and skirt. Almost as young as Mogs. Mogs was fatter than ever and she would soon be taller than Joan. Mogs was the only one of the party who was not cross and tired. She was wild with delight that they were here. Crazy to get unpacked, find her swimming suit and rush down to that inviting beach for a bathe.

Clare felt that she had chosen a good spot. Just before four o'clock they had come upon Kymer Cove suddenly, over the brow of a steep hill, then descended to the village down a long, twisting road. Bit by bit, the glories of the Cove had been unfolded to them. They had been lucky enough to arrive on a perfect afternoon. The village consisted of a cluster of small granite built cottages, a 'general store' and post office, and the hotel, which looked ultramodern and incongruous in such surroundings. In between two jutting headlands, the sea, a deeper blue than the sky, rolled into shore in long majestic breakers crested with the churned cream of the foam. The beach was sandy — that rich golden sand only to be found on the North Cornish coast. Against the sky, the jagged black rocks and tall cliffs looked almost violet, in a haze of sunlight. Half a mile from shore stood the famous Gull Rock, a solitary island, like a sentinel rising from the blue depths of the water. It was covered with sea pinks and samphire, and fluttering hosts of the grey, graceful birds from which it took its name.

The Tardys had felt the wind blowing

cool and pure against their faces as they descended the hill into Kymer village. A breeze full of the healthy tang of the Atlantic. Guy had said:

'By Jove, it looks a lovely place!'

Jack had said:

'There ought to be some good bass-fishing off those rocks.'

Mogs had been so excited and had said so many things that Clare couldn't remember one of them.

Only Joan said nothing. As though her first glimpse of Kymer Cove did not interest her. That was how she had been lately. So disinterested in everything and everybody. Clare, thinking about her family, made up her mind to speak to Jack about Joan. Perhaps Jack could get into her confidence and find out the trouble. Jack, himself, had been a bit depressed lately. Not been at all in his usual good form when he came down from Oxford this vacation. His face looked thin and he was working harder than was necessary. Perhaps something was not quite right with Jack. Secretly,

Clare worried about and brooded over all her children. She wanted them to be happy. She could not bear to see them looking miserable.

But if they had secrets from her, what could she do? Once upon a time, she had fondly imagined that they would always tell her everything. It was a mistake for any mother to imagine that. Mogs couldn't keep a secret, she had to blurt out everything. But that was how she was made. And she was only fourteen. When the children grew older, they became more reticent, more secretive. That was natural. They must eventually become individuals and have lives of their own. Jack and Joan were discovering their own personalities and did not wish to share the discovery with anyone, even their mother.

Clare did not blame them for having their secrets, but she wished, sometimes quite desperately, that they would let her share their sorrows.

Perhaps they said nothing because they thought her old-fashioned and feared that she might not understand them. If only they knew how young and modern she felt herself to be! If only they realized that she had by no means finished with life because she was their mother and forty two. That there was still plenty of time for her to make fresh discoveries about herself and about life. And that she could understand all that they yearned for — and all their illusions and disillusionments.

The hotel looked a grand place and did not fall far short of the flowery superlatives in the brochure which had praised it so highly. It was built almost on the edge of the cliff, on the right headland encircling the Cove. A wonderful position. As they drove in, the family had been quick to note the well-kept grass tennis courts, and pleasant gardens. A wooden stairway zigzagged down the cliff to the beach. The place had not long been built and therefore was of modern design and comfort. The lounge was charming. Green and cream colour scheme. Brown basket tables and chairs. Through the big, long, glass windows, the sun poured brilliantly. Afternoon tea was being served. Clare had visions of a heavenly meal with Cornish scones; 'splits' they called them, and thick yellow cream and jam. If only the manageress would hurry!

The place seemed a big improvement, anyhow, on that place in Cromer, where they had gone last year. Clare had just seen a nice looking girl, carrying a tennis racket, pass through the lounge with a boy of her own age. She was glad there were young people here for Jack and Joan.

Up shot the little glass partition, revealing the office. Miss Minter reappeared on the scene.

'I am extremely sorry, Mrs. Tardy, but I don't see what we can do about this mistake. We admit that it is ours . . . ' Miss Minter used the royal pronoun royally. 'But room Number Eleven, which should have been given to your son, is now occupied by a gentleman who is going to be here for a month. I don't quite see what we can do.'

Clare went a little pink in the cheeks. Her anger returned. After all the trouble she had taken to reserve the rooms so long ago, this seemed very deserving of her indignation. Of course there was the front double. But she wanted Guy to have that. He was the breadwinner of the family and should be considered. And as she must share it with him, that meant that they would have the only good view. The children would all have back windows. It was too bad. Clare continued to protest and argue with Miss Minter.

Miss Minter, raising her voice a little, said:

'But now the room has been given to Mr. Randall. We cannot very well take it away from him.'

'Did Mr. Randall book it?' inquired Clare icily.

'He booked *a* room,' began Miss Minter.

'And was given *my* room!'

'I'm sorry, Mrs. Tardy.'

'And I am sorry to insist,' broke in Clare. 'But I think Mr. Randall should be told — '

'Well, here he is,' said a man's pleasant voice behind her, 'if you want to tell him anything.'

Clare swung round. She saw a very tall man wearing white flannels and a silk tennis shirt. He was holding a racket and a net of tennis balls in one hand, and a half smoked cigarette in the other. So tall was he that she had to look up at him. He made her feel very short.

'Oh!' she gasped, embarrassed.

Blake Randall smiled at her. She amused him with that light of battle in her eyes and her brilliant flush of annoyance. A little angry woman, whose age he could not begin to judge. She might be anything between thirty and forty. He knew at once that he liked the look of her. How her eyes flashed! And very attractive brown eyes they were. Her silky dark hair escaped untidily from the brim of a small straw hat. She was dressed in pale green. A nice cool shade of green. Her voice was attractive, low-pitched. He liked dark-eyed women with low voices, and hated blondes with high-pitched screams. He went on smiling at the little, dark angry woman.

'What can I do for you? You were saying that I ought to be told something.'

'Well — I — it's all rather awkward,' stammered Clare.

Miss Minter cut in:

'I'm so sorry, Mr. Randall. I wouldn't have had this happen for worlds. But there has been a mistake and Mrs. Tardy booked Number Eleven, which we gave to you.'

Clare's anger evaporated. She had to smile at the change in the demeanour of Miss Minter. She had been a frozen spinster when addressing one of her own sex and was now a smiling, coy, gurgling female, blinking bashfully over her glasses at the tall Mr. Randall.

Clare put a finger to her lips.

That name was vaguely familiar. Randall. Where had she met a *Randall?* And now that she looked at him, this tall man was becoming familiar. Hadn't she seen him somewhere? He was not a person one would forget easily. Apart from his exceptional height — he must be at least six-foot-three — he had a striking face. Too gaunt and lined to be handsome. But a face one would look at twice. Very strongly moulded, and burnt a dark brown, as though he had been in the tropics. No English sun could have given him that depth of tan. In contrast, his hair was a pale grey and a little shaggy. His eyes were a curious colour, hazel with a lot of yellow in the iris. It was those eyes which awoke the memory in Clare. Of *course.* She knew who he was now.

She saw him suddenly — a boy in his twenties, with hair black as jet and those striking eyes looking at her from a dead-white face. A face which she had bent over in a hospital ward where she had been nursing as a V.A.D. just before she met Guy. She had thought, then, what curious eyes they were. They had been dark with pain. And the tall body had been stretched helplessly on a bed from which he was not to rise again for nine long months. His leg had been shattered. It hung suspended in a Thomas's splint. One of the worst fractured femur cases. Odd bits of bone had to be taken away, time and time again. He had operation after operation. Always very brave. And always gay. He had had a spice of the devil in him, young Captain Randall. Kept the ward alive with his stories, and the practical jokes which he liked to play on the Sisters when they bullied. But he was always kind to the young, overworked V.A.D.s.

Clare stood staring at him, her heart-beats beginning to quicken with excitement as the past came nearer and she saw it almost as though it were the present. Why, she had been teased about Captain Randall by the other nurses because he preferred her to do his dressings. He said she had particularly kind, clever hands, and that he suffered less pain from her touch than from any other nurse in the hospital.

Of *course!* Clare's brain worked furiously, remembering. Captain Randall was one of her earliest 'crushes'. (That made her think of Mogs.) She had suffered the pangs of unrequited love because he had flirted with all the pretty nurses. But one day when he was up on crutches, looking taller and paler than ever, and most attractive because of that air of delicacy, a lovely girl had come to see him. A chic young woman whom he introduced to them as his future wife. Thus had ended Clare's romance. Memory of him, too, had fled, when almost immediately after, Captain Randall was discharged from hospital, and Clare met Guy and married him.

Here was that very same Blake Randall whom she had not seen for so many long years. What an amazing coincidence that he should be at the Headland Hotel in Kymer Cove!

He was speaking to her, now.

'I'm frightfully sorry about this muddle. But it seems to me that if you booked the room so long ago, you ought to have it, and I'll move into the back.'

Then Clare said, quite irrelevantly:

'You *are* the Captain Randall whom I nursed at the Red Cross Hospital in Camberley, aren't you?'

He stared at her.

'Yes, indeed. Did you nurse me? What — what name?'

Her eyes sparkled at him.

'Don't you remember? Clare Wickham.'

He gave a gasp. His gaunt face creased into a smile of recognition and pleasure.

'Well, for heaven's sake! Little Wicks. Why, Lord above!'

Clare, pinker than ever, gave an excited laugh.

'That's right. And it was you who christened me 'Little Wicks'. It does bring back old days to hear that name.'

His hand shot out.

'Now I can see that it's you. You haven't really changed. You're just the same as ever.'

Her fingers were wrung in the large brown hand. She protested.

'Don't be so absurd! Of course I've changed! I'm the fat mother of three enormous children.'

'You may be the mother of the children, but I don't see the fat,' said he with a smile, releasing her fingers. 'I say, this *is* pleasant! I haven't met anybody from the old hospital for years — except Mortlake out in Persia last winter. Do you remember old Major Mortlake? Still in the Army and now a Brigadier. He asked if I'd ever heard of you again.'

'But of course you hadn't.'

'I may say,' added Blake Randall, 'Little Wicks was the only nurse old Mortlake *did* remember.'

'How sweet of him.'

'And what about that red-haired girl

who was your friend? Nurse Baines? Peggy? She was a grand person. Did you keep in touch?'

'She wrote just now and then,' said Clare. 'And as a matter of fact, she got married and went out to the Malay States and died there, poor dear.'

'How very sad. One can't think of that gay, amusing girl as dead. I'm glad you're still alive, Little Wicks.'

She shook her head, laughing.

'I just can't get over hearing that name. It brings back the whole life at the hospital. That ward. Matron. Our concerts. What fun we had, and how marvellous you all were, in spite of your frightful wounds.'

He tapped his right leg.

'Still got it, you see. In fact, I haven't had any trouble since that last operation at Camberley. Pretty lucky. Just a bit of a limp. It doesn't even stop me playing games.'

'Or dancing? Do you remember how afraid you were that you wouldn't be able to dance? You always said it was your favourite occupation.'

'It still is. And you were a pretty useful dancer, yourself, Wicks. I remember watching you on the night we had our big party. I was furious because I couldn't join in, and wished to God I'd been hit in the arm instead of the leg. You were the best dancer among all the nurses.'

'Oh, dear!' sighed Clare. 'Just imagine!'

And she needed some imagination, to believe that she had ever been the best dancer in any room. Guy didn't dance. She hadn't danced for years. But she had loved it. She could so well remember that party night at the hospital to which Blake Randall had referred. And how heart-broken she had been because her favourite Captain was on crutches and couldn't put an arm around her. And how teased she had been for sitting out with him. He had stolen a kiss, that night.

Lord! It couldn't be true that this tall man standing in front of her was the young wounded officer whose fleeting caress had roused such intense excitement in her young heart. Intense was the word. One suffered then as only the very young can suffer. She had been just about Joan's age. Perhaps a year older. And because of the war and its unnatural excitement, they had all been so keyed up that they had taken their joys and sorrows much more seriously than one took them in more normal times. She had not forgotten his kiss for a long while. Then, when Guy came on the scene and her sentimental young heart had begun to beat for him and respond to his quiet, serious courtship, both Blake Randall and her fervour for him had faded into obscurity. Yet it all came back poignantly today as she looked at him. And here she was, aged forty-two and the mother of those tall children out there on the porch. Blake Randall must be older than herself. He was completely grey.

'It seems like yesterday,' she said.

'And yet it seems part of another life altogether.'

The acid voice of Miss Minter interrupted. It had obviously brought her no relief from her worries to know that these two had met before.

'Might we just settle about this room . . . ?'

Clare turned to her.

'It doesn't matter at all. My son must have the back room. We wouldn't dream of turning Captain Randall out.'

'No longer 'Captain',' said Blake. 'I dropped that title when I left the Army after the Armistice. And by the way, what is your name now? Of course it's 'Little Wicks' no more.'

'Mrs. Tardy,' said Clare. 'My husband is Dr. Tardy. He and my family are out there.' She nodded toward the open doors.

Blake Randall turned and saw the little group silhouetted against the brilliant light. He had noticed them as he came in. Particularly the slim, pretty girl with reddish-brown curls.

'Those can't be your children — that young man with the golf-clubs — that great girl!'

'They are,' laughed Clare. 'Which shows you how time has passed.'

'My God!' said Blake Randall, in a voice of dismay. 'It makes me feel decrepit. I remember in hospital, I was older than you by five years.'

'Well, there you are. What do you think it makes me feel like?'

'I only know what you look like. I refuse to believe you're their mother. You must have adopted them.'

Clare beamed. It was really nice to get a spontaneous compliment like that. She was suddenly proud of the fact that she had kept her slim lines. The mere sight of Blake Randall, and the past which he evoked, made her feel younger than she had felt for a very long while. Not at all decrepit.

Blake Randall went on looking down at her intensely. He had always been a great admirer of Little Wicks. She had been an extremely pretty child in her

V.A.D. uniform. And a damn good nurse. Vivacious, too. She had whiled away many hours of pain and boredom for him with her buoyant youth and tender ministrations. And she was still very pretty. The child had become a charming looking woman.

It couldn't be possible that she was mother to that family. And what on earth had she seen to love in that queer, little, half-bald, unromantic man? A doctor, was he? Well, he looked anything but the answer to the prayer of a romantic girl. Women were strange creatures. There was no knowing what attracted them. He had seen the most lovely girls marry the dullest, plainest fellows. At the same time, he had a faint and pleasant recollection that Little Wicks had once had a distinct penchant for himself. But at that time, flirting with all women, he had only loved one. The one he had married. He banished her memory quickly because it hurt. He said:

'No more arguments about the room.

I'm moving out and your boy's got to move in. It's only right.'

'No, please . . . ' began Clare.

'I've made up my mind,' he said. 'Miss Minter, please have my things moved and let Mrs. Tardy have the room which she booked.'

'It's awfully nice of you, and quite unnecessary,' said Clare.

'I don't really mind where I sleep,' he smiled down at her.

'Well, I don't think Jack would mind, either.'

'Is that your boy?'

'Yes. He's up at Oxford. Studying Law.'

'And the girl?'

'Joan's eighteen and at home. Mogs is still at school.'

'Is Mogs that young thing with the dimples and red curls? Looks a jolly kid.'

'You must meet them all. It's such fun your being down here. We're here for three weeks.'

They began to move away from the

office, through the lounge. And now Clare noticed Blake Randall's very slight limp. She noticed, too, when the strong light struck his face, that he had changed greatly from the gay, carefree boy of the hospital days. There was tragedy written on his face today. He was telling her that he had been ill. He had got some strange fever abroad. He was always abroad — general sales-manager for the Milestone Petrol Company. That was a very big job, Clare thought, and must carry a handsome salary. Milestone Petrol was popular. In fact, they used it for their own car.

Randall was down here for a month's recuperation before going abroad again. That meant they would be able to see a lot of each other and talk over old times to their hearts' content. Clare felt a warm, pleasurable little sensation. Usually, the family holiday meant that she was very much alone. Guy either went fishing with Jack or slept the hours away. The girls had their own companions and pursuits. If she wanted company, Clare had, as a rule, to talk to some other 'mother' or middle-aged woman in the hotel. And it was dull, *dull*, talking of nothing but servants and the family. It would be wonderful to have a friend of the war who could share with her countless interesting reminiscences. Especially this man, who had been such a favourite in her girlhood.

It was on the tip of her tongue to ask him if he had married the beautiful fiancée who had visited him during the war. Then she desisted. Perhaps the wife was the tragedy. Perhaps she had died. Later he would be sure to tell her.

She saw Guy and Jack coming toward them and prepared to introduce her old friend to the family.

2

Joan, kneeling in front of Mogs' school trunk in which both their things had been packed for the holiday, took out a bright blue bathing-suit and flung it at her young sister. Mogs, sitting on the edge of the bed removing shoes and stockings, said:

'Thanks. Blast! I've torn a hole.'

Joan looked over her shoulder.

'Do be careful. You know Mum says I've got to do half the darning. You jolly well ought to darn your own things, now you're nearly fifteen.'

Mogs pulled her vest over her head. She snorted sarcastically.

'Fifteen when I'm wanted for anything useful. Only fourteen when it's whether I should stay up at nights or not.'

Joan made no answer but continued to unpack. She had to smile a little.

Mogs always said such funny things. But it was a sad little smile which curved Joan's mouth, and she banished it quickly almost as though she felt she had no right to smile. She was so unhappy. She couldn't, *couldn't* get over Anthony. And it was really the limit that when they reached Kymer and drove into the hotel, the first thing she saw was a yew on the front lawn, clipped to the shape of a fox. The hotel crest, on every sheet of notepaper, was a *fox*. As if she hadn't enough to remind her of Tony without that (Oh, poor Little Fox!)

Mogs, in her bathing-suit, pattered on bare feet across the room.

'Chuck me my bath-gown.'

Joan rose from her knees.

'Find it for yourself, ducks,' she said wearily.

Mogs dived into the trunk.

'Isn't this a *super* hotel? Doesn't the bathing look *gorgeous*? I must ask them downstairs for a surf-board. Why don't you come with me, Joaney?'

'I'll bathe tomorrow,' said Joan.

'Chris is coming the day after tomorrow, isn't he?'

'Yes.'

'I've got a crush on Chris.'

Another faint smile on Joan's lips. She lit a cigarette.

'And what about Miss Walters?'

'I've gone off her. She was jolly mean last term. When I made a mistake at the concert in my piece, she told Miss Crockford that I'd had plenty of time to practise and that I'd been lazy.'

'I expect you had.'

'You *would* say that! Anyhow, even if it was true, it was jolly rotten of her to say it, when she knew how keen I was on her. I had an awful lot of disappointments last term.'

'Poor Moggy!'

Joan was sorry the child had had disappointments. Lord knew, she was facing plenty more. It seemed to Joan that life was made up of disappointments. She only hoped that Mogs would never, *never* meet an Anthony

Downe. How anybody could be so charming, so heartless, so clever and *beastly!*

'I think Chris is a poppet,' said Mogs. 'And awfully good-looking, don't you agree?'

'Yes.'

'I wish I wasn't so young. He might have had a crush on me. He said Titian would have raved about my hair. And he's going to do a lovely painting of me sitting on the rocks combing my locks, like a mermaid.'

'Not much mermaid about you, cherub,' said Joan with a derisive look at Mogs' generous curves.

'Beast!' said Mogs. 'Just because you're so thin! And you know Chris has got a crush on *you!'*

Joan, cigarette between her lips, and cheeks a slightly heightened colour, walked to one of the windows which opened out on to a little wooden balcony. For a moment she shut her eyes. The sun was warm on her upturned face. Comforting. And there was something soothing in the rhythmic sibilant hiss of the water breaking on the shore. She could hear it even though their room faced the back garden and tennis-courts.

She thought of a Swinburne poem which she and Tony had once read together. The anguished cry of the unrequited lover.

'I will go back to the great, sweet
    mother,
Mother and lover of men, the
    sea . . .
Save me and hide me with all thy
    waves
Find me one grave of thy thou-
    sand graves . . . '

That's what she felt like. These last few weeks had been so terrible. She had missed Anthony and all that Anthony had meant with a pain which she had felt was beyond bearing. She would like to run down to that sea, be immersed in it, and let it wash away remembrance.

People would call that hysteria. Perhaps it was! Chris would have another word for it. Cowardice! Chris was a very brave person. She had learnt many things about him during their growing friendship. What a lot of ill-health he had had to combat as a boy, and even at Oxford. Some slight spinal trouble which caused him frequent pain. He was now in the hands of a marvellous osteopath who was curing him. None of them had ever known about his bad spine, until he had told her. These days, Joan was aware of the indomitable courage in that slender, fair-haired young man with his artist's soul. It made her ashamed. She had been so very cowardly over Anthony. Just gone to pieces! The only brave thing she had done was to keep the secret from her mother and the others. And that was mainly because she dreaded becoming an object of general pity. Somehow she didn't mind Chris pitying her. She had told him everything.

Had Mogs' childish, tactless words any truth in them? Had Chris got 'a crush' on her? She didn't know, of course. He was frightfully sweet to her, but she didn't think it was that . . .

Today, she began to ask herself if, perhaps, there was more than she knew at the back of the young artist's comradeship? The look in the eye. An extra pressure of the hand. A suggestion of some feeling not altogether platonic? It gave her to think. It would be so queer. Why, Chris had been friends with Jack for two years and she had never really liked him. But now she liked him very much and admired him, too. She began to feel glad that he was coming down for the holiday. After all, it was such a strain always having to act for the family. It would be a relief to have someone with her with whom she could be *herself*.

She turned back to the room. It was not a bad room. Everything was fresh and new. The blue and white curtains and bed-covers were in quite good taste. There was an electric fire, and a basin with running-water.

Mogs struggled with a white rubber bathing-cap which refused to encompass her head of thick curls.

'Oh, blast! It *does* stick.'

'Let me help, darling.'

Mogs' eyes, periwinkle blue, danced at her sister.

'Lord! You are being nice! You've been frightfully nice ever since I came home. I think you must be going into a decline and dying, like Greta Garbo in 'Camille'.'

'Anybody would think I'd been horrid to you before.'

'No, but you *are* miles nicer now. Only Mum's worrying because she thinks you're ill.'

Joan bit her lip.

'I'm all right.'

'I believe you have fallen in love with somebody.'

'Oh, Mogs, do be quiet and let me help you with your cap.'

'Everybody's gone funny,' continued

Mogs. 'Jack's as grim as he can be. What's happened to him?'

Joan flung her cigarette-end out of the window. She didn't know much more than Mogs what was wrong with Jack. She only knew that he never mentioned his girlfriend now. When he came down in June, she had asked him how Amanda was, and he had returned the pound she had lent him and said:

'Oh, that's all finished.'

Which meant, of course, that he had had a quarrel with the girl. But she couldn't possibly believe that Jack's affair was as bad as her own had been. It *couldn't* be.

'I say, Joan,' continued Mogs, with her love of chatter. 'What do you think of Mummy's boyfriend?'

'Don't be vulgar, Mogs. Mummy hasn't got a 'boyfriend'.'

'Well, that huge individual with the shaggy head whom she said she'd nursed in the war?'

'Oh! I think he looks rather nice.'

'I believe Mummy had a crush on

291

him when she was young.'

'You and your crushes! For heaven's sake go and swim.'

'I shall make Pop come with me.'

Mogs, wearing rope-soled sandals, her striped orange wrap over her shoulders, and joy in her heart, went in search of her father.

Joan continued to unpack. Having done so, she changed from her suit into a pair of linen trousers and cotton shirt, and tucked a bright red scarf in the neck. These were her last summer's trousers. Two inches too big in the waist. She had to draw them in tightly with a belt. No wonder Mum worried about her, losing so much weight. She would have to try and eat a lot of cream and bread and try to get back some flesh. If only she could feel happy again! She used to grumble a lot and think home-life dull and the family sticky. The life which Anthony had shown her had dazzled her. Blinded her. And now it didn't seem as though she could see straight any more. But she did know that she had been happier before Anthony came.

Mummy had chosen a lovely place. It might have been so grand. But she couldn't get away from the stinging memory of Tony's derision. This was the beginning of what he called the 'beach and blister' holiday. Damn him! *Damn* him, for having taught her to love him in that subtle, insinuating way of his.

Outside the door, she could hear Mogs' high, excited voice:

'Hurry and change, then, Daddy. I'll wait for you downstairs.'

Lucky Mogs! Her disappointment in Miss Walters hadn't counted for much. Her volatile spirits soon soared. Her 'crush' on Chris meant nothing but a pleasant piece of sentiment — someone to adore. Happy Mogs!

Joan sat down on one of the twin beds, put her face against the cool pillow and cried helplessly. She cried, although she knew that there was every chance that her mother would come in and find her thus and be horrified. But she couldn't help it. And it struck her, even while she cried, that it was not altogether because she was still in love with Anthony Downe. She wasn't. She despised him. But she was still in love with *love* and all the glamour of it which he had taken from her during that last wretched scene with him.

The bedroom door opened. It was what she had feared. Somebody had come in. Too late for her to sit up and dry her tears, so she just went on lying there with her face hidden.

It was with some relief that she heard her brother's voice.

'I say, Joaney — what's up?'

She could not answer. She felt Jack sit on the bed beside her and put an arm around her shoulders.

'Joan, old girl, what's wrong? I say, don't cry like that! What is it?'

She sobbed into the pillow:

'Oh, Jack, I'm so miserable!'

'I know you are. And so'm I, if it comes to that. We seem a pretty pair.

There's some fellow in it, isn't there, Joan? That dress-designer.'

Up shot Joan's head and she turned a wet, disfigured face to her brother.

'Who told you?'

'Don't be an ass! Nobody. I guessed it. You've been going round with those Downes. You know Mum was worried stiff about you. But she never said anything. She's so grand like that.'

Joan drew a handkerchief from the pocket of her trousers and wiped her eyes.

'I know she is.'

'Well, why don't you tell me, Joan? Perhaps I could help.'

'Nobody could.'

'That's a bit how I feel. But sometimes it gets one down not being able to talk to anybody.'

'As a matter of fact, I've told Chris.'

Jack took a packet of cigarettes from his pocket and lit one.

'I guessed that, too. I'm rather glad you and old Chris are becoming pals. But I feel a bit hurt that you haven't included me in your confidence.'

'Why should I? You haven't included me in yours,' said Joan, with a flash of the old sisterly spirit.

Jack looked moodily through the window.

'I haven't told a soul. I felt much too rotten about it.'

Joan blew her nose forlornly.

'We might as well tell each other now, mightn't we?'

'Okay! I will if you will.'

Two pairs of young, miserable eyes looked into each other. Solemnly, brother and sister sat on the bed, each unfolding a story of personal misery and defeat. Yet, in Joan's case, not altogether of defeat, but victory. A victory won over herself.

'You see how it was with me, Jack. I couldn't do what he asked. I know it was old-fashioned in his eyes, suburban and all the rest of it. But what would Mum and Dad have done if anything had happened to me?'

Jack, scowling, smoking, said:

'I think you were damn right. The man was a bastard to ask you, and I'd like to go and knock his ruddy head off.'

Joan squeezed his arm.

'It's sweet of you, but that wouldn't help matters.'

'You were damned right,' repeated Jack, 'and I must say I admire you for it enormously. Poor kid, it must have been rotten for you, ending that way. Were you very keen?'

'Yes.'

'So was I — on Amanda.'

'Well, of course — from what you've told me about *her*, I think she ought to be boiled in oil,' said Joan hotly. 'I've never heard of *anybody* behaving so badly.'

'I told her what I thought of her that night,' said Jack in his grimmest voice.

Joan gave a deep sigh.

'My God! We do seem to have chosen foul people to love.'

'I don't love Amanda any more. I hate her memory. What's made me miserable is feeling that she was the first with me. I didn't behave as well as you, Joan.'

'Oh, well, it's different for a man,' said Joan loyally.

'Can you imagine,' he added, 'what Mother would have said if I'd brought Amanda down from Oxford and introduced her as my wife, and then we'd found out all that business about her kid and her age.'

'It would have broken Mummy's heart.'

'Well, that's the only good thing that's come out of this muck. Mum's been spared from knowing about either of us.'

'She's so sweet and good to us. I'm glad nothing drastic happened to hurt her.'

Jack got up and wandered round the room.

'You don't ever hear from that fellow now?'

'He did write once. Asked me to go and see him again and said he was sorry for what he'd done.'

'All he wanted was your lily-white body, my child.'

'I know that. I've learnt a lot. And I didn't go. Do you hear from Amanda?'

'I've had about twenty-four letters and chucked them all in the fire. Except one, from her sister Sheila, telling me that I was a swine and that I'd ruined her sister's life. I sent that back with *'Oh yeah!'* written at the bottom of it.'

Joan went to the wash-basin and began to sluice her face with spongefuls of cold water.

'I'm awfully sorry, Jack. It must have been horrible for you.'

'Well, I've finished with women!' said Jack, and added: 'At least for years! Perhaps I'll marry when I'm thirty.'

'I don't think I shall ever marry,' said Joan.

Then Jack grinned at her.

'I bet you do.'

A knock on the door and their mother's voice:

'Joan! Are you there, dear?'

'Go — and say I'll be down in a minute, Jack. I don't want her to see my face until I've made it up.'

'It's not such a bad face,' said Jack, and dropped a kiss upon Joan's hair, which left her strangely comforted.

While she rubbed foundation-cream into her cheeks, she thought a lot about Jack and how nice he was, and what a rotten thing it was for a creature like this Amanda to have got hold of him. She also thought that it was a pity that people like Anthony and Amanda couldn't meet and give each other hell. But of course they'd have no mutual appeal. They'd see through each other too quickly!

Suddenly Joan found herself whistling under her breath. The first time she had whistled or felt at all light-hearted since she had run away from Anthony Downe's flat. That cry and that talk with Jack had done her quite a lot of good. And Chris was coming the day after tomorrow. She looked forward to seeing Chris . . .

3

Clare Tardy sat on a bathing-wrap upon the beach, with her back against a sun-warmed rock, and looked out to sea. Blake Randall was beside her. Some way away, sheltered from the blistering sun, Guy Tardy lay sleeping soundly after his three o'clock dip. Joan, Jack, Chris and Mogs had taken the car and gone for a picnic-lunch into Newquay. They were expected back to tea.

Said Clare:

'I can't believe we've been here two whole weeks, Blake. They've simply flown!'

'They certainly have,' said Blake Randall. 'And up till now, I may say that this fortnight's been one of the most pleasant I've ever spent in my life.'

'I agree,' said Clare softly.

She took off her dark glasses for a

moment, shut her eyes and sighed for pure pleasure. She liked to hear Blake Randall speak of this holiday as though he had enjoyed it. Every night when she went to bed, she wondered whether she was enjoying it too much, or had been over-appreciative of the renewal of their war friendship.

Taking it all round, the holiday was being a success. Dear old Guy never enthused wildly about anything, but he was getting as much sun and rest as he wanted. They had been marvellously lucky with the weather. And the inclusion of Chris Fenlick in the party had proved popular.

Thinking of the family, Clare was mainly relieved because of the change in Joan. Even in this short fortnight the girl had put on a little weight. She was growing brown and looking much happier. Mogs, in one of her chattering moods, had said that she thought Joan and Chris were 'keen'. Well, nothing pleased Clare more than to think that Joan should become interested in Jack's friend. The more she saw of the young artist, the more she liked him.

And thinking of herself, Clare knew that this meeting with Blake Randall had made all the difference to her own enjoyment. There had been no boring, solitary hours for her, this holiday. If Guy went off on a whole day's fishing, or dozed and read, Blake Randall was always there — ready to talk to her and amuse her. He was always amusing. He still retained that inimitable sense of humour which he had shown in hospital days. And it was something new for Clare to have a real attendant. Someone who seemed to like to wait on her, to carry things for her down to the beach, to change a book for her at the library, to surprise her with little gifts of flowers or fruit, tins of thick Cornish cream, or expensive magazines which she would never have dreamed of buying for herself.

Someone who seemed to think that *she* was the one person in the family to be considered. And last, but not least, someone who regarded her not merely as the mother of the family, settled and finished, but as a woman to be admired. A woman to be a little flattered. Why, when she put on a nice dress now, she knew that it would be noticed and appreciated. Blake Randall would give a word of praise. He never stopped telling her how absurdly young she looked to be the mother of a boy like Jack. Indeed, he was making her quite conceited. By the time he had finished, she would have a swollen head. And by the time he had finished, he might do something even more dangerous . . . make her discontented with her lot. That would be fatal!

She had known, of course, for years that Guy was not the lover and companion she should have chosen. But she had accepted that fact and immersed herself in her family duties and pleasures. She did not want to be made conscious of any real gaps or needs. And this man frightened her. In some strange way he brought her face to face with every deficiency in her life. He said nothing about it. Of course he wouldn't. He admired Guy. He and Guy had had some talks, and Blake had told her how clever he thought Guy was on his own subjects. He adored the children. They liked him, too. They had become friends. And even Guy had said, only last night:

'A very decent fellow, Randall.'

A lot from Guy!

No, Blake Randall would never have pointed out even indirectly that she had married the wrong man or made a mistake. Yet, when she was with him, especially when they were alone, he forced upon her mysteriously the knowledge that she was not in her element in the family circle. But with him, she became the real Clare. That gay, impetuous Clare of the glowing colours. She remembered how she had put away Guy's tie one day and thought how grey everything was about him. There was nothing grey about Blake Randall. He was a radiant, colourful personality.

They had such long, exciting talks. Not only about hospital days, but about themselves. She knew quite a lot about him now.

He led a glamorous existence, travelling to the far places of the world on behalf of his company. Often in the air, flying here, and there. He had an inexhaustible fund of stories. His experiences in China, in Africa, in Europe. He had been in revolutions. He was one of the last Britishers to be evacuated by battleship from Southern Spain. He had been as near death recently from revolutionary bullets as in the Great War where he had got his leg-wound.

He loved his life — enjoyed every minute of it. Behind the gaunt, grey man there was still the boy whose torch of adventurous youth burned bravely. He had met people of every race. He had had his love-affairs — he told Clare about some of them. Breathless, romantic stories. And he told her of the one

306

deathless romance. Deathless, although *she*, his wife, had died. He had married that beautiful girl who, Clare remembered, had visited him in hospital. They had had five matchless years together. Then his son had been born and death had taken both mother and child. That was the tragedy which had sent his hair grey overnight and carved those deep lines on his face.

To Clare, he had spoken freely of Helen and the days they had spent together. Clare knew that the other loves had not mattered, that it was because of Helen's memory that he had never married again. She knew, too, that he was lonely. He had devoted his life to his job. But a job is a poor mistress for any man. He needed a real home and the wife who had been taken from him.

'It may be silly of me,' he had said to Clare, when speaking of Helen, 'but every time I've considered re-marrying, something has stopped me. Almost a feeling that it would be an act of disloyalty to *her*. Damn foolish, I admit. But she was mine as no other woman could ever be, and I was hers. I just couldn't give anybody else that name which she had borne.'

And he told Clare, that he felt, rightfully or wrongfully, that he was responsible for Helen's death. He should never have let her have that child. When Clare had tried to comfort him and disburden his soul of that particular grief, he had cried:

'Oh, I know! I wasn't to blame any more than any other man who has children. How should I know that everything would go wrong? It's a chance in ten thousand. But I can never forgive myself, when I look back and think that if it hadn't been for the child, she would still be living. She was so young — so lovely when she died.'

Clare had said:

'I'm unutterably sorry for you, Blake. But I don't think you must complain if you have had even five years of real happiness. It isn't given to everybody to experience perfect love and comrade-ship. You say you had both with your Helen. My God . . . ' And she had added, before she could restrain herself: 'How I envy you!'

He had looked at her from his curious, tawny eyes, full of understand-ing, and whispered:

'Why! Poor little Wicks!'

And that had made her feel like a stupid, emotional schoolgirl and she had been awfully ashamed of herself and of the disloyalty to Guy which had lain behind her simple words. Blake Randall must know that she had meant that she, herself, had never experienced the perfect happiness which had been his.

When they were alone, he still called her 'Little Wicks'. She found the nickname very pleasing and reminiscent of their old, happy friendship in Camberley. When with the family, they were 'Clare' and 'Blake' to each other. The only time 'Little Wicks' had slipped out before the children, Mogs had howled with laughter; thought it a tremendous joke.

'Mummy as 'Little Wicks',' she had giggled. 'It *does* sound a scream. I can't imagine it!'

No, these children of hers couldn't imagine her as the girl she had been. And Guy had forgotten. He had grown old with her and did not mind growing older. But Blake Randall thought of her and treated her still as the young nurse of the war. Perhaps, she told herself, she was an old fool to enjoy it so much. But there was no gainsaying the fact that she did.

Blake Randall pulled a packet of cigarettes from the pocket of the grey flannel trousers which he wore over his bathing-suit.

'Smoke?' he asked Clare.

'After our swim, I think. We're going in in a moment, aren't we?'

'Do you feel like a second one before tea?'

'I do indeed. I feel fine — never better in my life.'

He lit a cigarette for himself, flung the burnt match away, and gave Clare a sidelong smile.

'You look a marvel,' he said. 'As I've so many times told you, you *are* a complete marvel! You, the mother of that great family!'

'You're making me so vain, Blake, that I shall start agreeing with you soon and think that I *am* a marvel.'

And she said it with that warm, contented little feeling which a woman only experiences when she knows she is looking her best. This fortnight of complete rest, of sea and sunbathing, and happy companionship, had made a new creature of Clare. She not only looked young, but *felt* young again. She had played a good deal of tennis with Blake and with the children. Her muscles had hardened. She was slimmer and she was brown — with that rich tan that only a real brunette can achieve.

It was years since she had been conscious of her body as she was conscious of it now. She was proud of her long straight legs and tapering ankles. They were almost as good as Joan's! Of course, she hadn't Joan's small waist. But then, she had a son of twenty! And as for the tummy . . . well, she couldn't expect *that* to be as flat as a young girl's. But it wasn't too bad.

She was alive and glowing, which was such a change from the tired, negative Clare of London. She felt every morning when she woke up and got out of bed, that there were golden days full of promise to look forward to. In town there was nothing exciting. But there had never been such a holiday as this! And so much of it was due to Blake. Well, the one thing that frightened her, was the knowledge that in a week's time it would all be over.

Feeling Blake's gaze upon her, she was suddenly stricken with embarrassment and pulled a comb from the pocket of the flowered cretonne coat which she wore over a cherry-coloured swim-suit. She ran the comb through the sleek, dark waves of her hair. Hair still wet from the sea. She had never found a cap that kept out the water.

The man beside her was thinking that not since his wife died, had he been more attracted by any woman than by Clare Tardy. There was so much sweetness in her face and so much strength. He did not admire the unlined, characterless faces of the young women of today. They were painted masks. Even young Joan Tardy put far too much stuff on her face for his liking. But Clare's face was full of character. She used only lipstick — a very pleasant touch of red on that charming mouth. Her tanned skin was clear and smooth. And if there were shadows under her eyes, a tiny network of wrinkles that age had wrought, and those two tell-tale little lines which run from the corner of the mouth downwards, remorseless trace of the passing years, he liked them.

She was always happy and smiling, and doing things for other people — in

313

his opinion, doing too many things for that egotistical family of hers! She never whined or complained. But at the back of those hazel eyes lay suffering and repression. He had not watched her and talked with her for two whole weeks without knowing that life had cheated her.

Certainly, she had a very decent, honest-to-God sort of fellow for a husband. Blake was sure the doctor was the most loyal and dependable kind of chap. And those children were corking. God! He'd have given his soul to have a son like Jack. (Helen's boy might have been like Jack had he lived!) But a husband and a family weren't enough for a woman. Helen used to say so. Helen, young though she was, had been very wise and understanding about her sex. She used to tell him that the reason why he made her so happy was because he never forgot to be the lover as well as the husband. That was the desire of every woman's heart. To keep her lover and the glamour of being loved.

There was nothing glamorous about that stolid doctor who lay sleeping serenely behind the rocks. He must have forgotten long since how to flirt with his own wife. His job was mistress enough for him. And Blake Randall thought:

'Fool! Fool! With this sweet person who was made for love and loving! What a ghastly waste! She's still too young and romantic at heart to be turned into housekeeper and mother. If Helen had lived — had lived with me for twenty years, as this man has lived with this woman — she would still be to me the girl I loved with all the madness of my youth!'

Clare finished combing her hair and smiled at him.

'You're very serious today, Blake.'

'Just thinking,' he said briefly.

'What about?'

'You, as a matter of fact.'

'What about me?'

'All kinds of things.'

'Tell me some of them.'

'Tell me what you think lies in front of you these next few years.'

Clare blinked and replaced her sun-glasses and looked a moment without speaking out to sea. A slight breeze was churning the waves. They were breaking, white with foam, against the rocks. A gull, white and shining, with a fish in its beak, soared into the air and was followed by a dozen others. They wheeled and screamed, filling the air with their harsh complaint.

She said:

'Goodness! What a question to answer. What lies in front of me these next few years? I wonder! At a guess, I should say hard work helping the family make their way without letting them feel too much that they're being helped.'

He nodded, arms folded across his chest, cigarette between his lips, an old straw hat which he had bought in Malaya, tilted to shade his eyes.

'That's where you're such a clever mother, Little Wicks. You never let any

316

of them see what you're doing. Yet they all do pretty much what you want.'

'They're all very sweet.'

'That girl's not too easy, eh?'

'Joan has moods. But she's much better than she used to be. This holiday is making a big difference to her. She was worrying me very much in town. Getting in with the wrong set, and, I fancy, into the hands of a certain young gentleman who designs clothes. He was doing her no good at all.'

'She's pretty. A pretty daughter is bound to be a responsibility.'

'Yes. But I think she's got her head screwed on the right way. I don't believe she'd ever let me down.'

'Well, you wouldn't let her down.'

Clare coloured.

'I'd try not to.'

'Then let me tell you, you're very much more beautiful than she is.'

'Blake, really,' protested Clare. She was blushing to the roots of her hair. 'You're just as bad as you used to be in the hospital — you old flatterer!'

'It isn't flattery, Wicks. I do think you've grown into a very beautiful woman and you were one of the prettiest girls I'd ever seen.'

'I can't cope with you,' she laughed.

'Well, your Joan is all right. But I don't think she'll make the woman you are.'

'Give her a chance.'

'Is she keen on young Fenlick?'

'I hope and believe so. I'm devoted to Chris. We all are. Nothing would please me better than to see Joan marry Chris. But there's plenty of time. I don't want her to marry too young. I really couldn't face being a grandmother yet!'

'Grandmother my foot! It doesn't make sense — Little Wicks as a granny. No, we just can't allow Joan to marry yet.'

She smiled at him. Really, he was a darling! She recollected vaguely having had a similar conversation with Guy. Guy had taken it as a matter of course that they would soon become grandparents. And it hadn't mattered to him.

But Blake could see things from a woman's point of view — he could see that she didn't want to grow old and, having brought up one family, face the prospect of helping to bring up Joan's or Jack's! And in time, Mogs'! Could one imagine that dumpling growing up and getting married?

'Oh!' she said, with sudden passion. 'For Joan's sake, I don't want her to marry yet. I married when I was too young. A woman doesn't know her own mind until she's at least twenty-four or five.'

'And does she know it then?'

'Perhaps she never does. But she's more capable of judging who would or would not be the right man for her to marry.'

They were both silent after that. Perhaps both of them were thinking about Clare's choice. That man who was asleep behind the rocks.

Then Clare said hurriedly:

'Well, to return to this prospect of my

future. I shall have Joan to look after. Jack has got another year at Oxford before his finals. Then he's got to be launched in my brother-in-law's office. Moggie will be at school for the next three years, and then she'll go abroad.'

'And that's the prospect, eh?'

'It's full of interest.'

'Is it the sort of interest that means complete fulfilment for a woman?'

That gave her a sense of shock. Having asked herself that question a hundred times during her twenty-one years of marriage, it seemed rather dreadful to hear it so frankly spoken. Her reply was evasive.

'Oh — I don't know.'

But he knew. And he was suddenly angry. With Clare, for submitting so passively to her existence. With Guy Tardy, for missing the chance which he had had with this woman and pursuing his own work, his own course of life, with such sublime unconsciousness of his wife's needs. With those children, who expected everything of her as their mother and yet, every time, would put her aside for someone else . . . And with himself, because he was on the verge of interfering in somebody else's life. Interfering, not merely because he resented the thing for this woman's sake, but because he knew he would give so much to be in Guy Tardy's shoes today.

Clare attracted him in countless ways. She was not for an hour's light amusement, as others in his life had been. She was a woman whom he could have loved in the way that he had loved Helen, if not as much.

She had all the qualities which he admired and none of the drawbacks that he dreaded. Being honest with himself, he had to admit that this fortnight of watching her with husband and children, and spending so much time with her, had had a very profound effect upon him. And if she had not been another man's wife, she might have been the one woman in the world whom he would ask to take Helen's long vacated place.

Clare, with her sweet unselfishness, her kindness, her humour, had shown him how lonely he was, how much in need of all that she might have given. She had physical appeal for him — but so much more — they were friends. Just as they had been in the days when she nursed him. It was as though the long years between had never been.

He heard Clare say:

'When you've finished your cigarette, let's bathe.'

He flung his cigarette-end away and rose to his feet. He knew that she was anxious to avoid further discussion about herself. And that, more than anything, showed him how well and truly he had hit the mark.

Clare, with mingled feelings, took off her wrap and walked with him down to the sea. She thought:

'I oughtn't to let anything he says affect me. I oughtn't to dread the idea of saying goodbye to him next week.'

She said, with deliberate cheerfulness:

'What about *your* future, Blake? Are you going abroad again straight away?'

'Yes,' he said, with a grimness that he was still feeling.

'Where?'

'Oh, I think the firm wants me to go to Canada. And I may come back via the States and California.'

'Oh! Aren't you lucky!'

He gave her a sudden smile.

'You'd better come with me.'

'Oh, certainly!' she mocked. 'In what capacity, secretary or nurse? Is the leg going to break out again, so that I can stick on a white veil and apron and call myself Nurse Wickham?'

'I'm not sure what the Milestone Petrol Company in Canada would do if I turned up with a pretty nurse.'

'Oh, there'd be no scandal! I'm no girl,' she laughed. 'And I can easily bleach my hair white.'

'That wouldn't make you look a day older.'

'Then I'll have to refuse the job, Mr. Randall, and lose a nice trip to Canada, the States and California.'

They had reached the edge of the sea. They took off their shoes and threw them on to a rock. Clare, with that white rubber cap strapped under her chin looked younger than ever, he thought. He said:

'I wish I thought you could take that trip with me, Little Wicks. What fun we'd have.'

'I'm sure we would,' she said honestly.

Then their eyes met. And the look that she saw in his gave her the strangest tremor. She thought:

'Good heavens! We can't do this sort of thing. At least I can't, at my age. What would the family think?'

And turning away from Blake Randall's gaze, she looked out to the horizon. She found that her eyes were blinded as though by the sun. And she tried to fill her mind with all kinds of ordinary mundane things. Before dinner she must darn that hole in Jack's black silk evening socks. And she had promised to wash Joan's hair tonight, because it was full of sand and so sticky from bathing. What did Guy want? Nothing. He never did want much. It was awful to think how little her husband had been in the scheme of things during this holiday. She hardly saw him. They shared the same bedroom, but when they lay in their beds, they only talked for a few minutes, then they slept. That was marriage with Guy. What would it have been like with Blake Randall? His wife must have adored him. He had the most compelling personality . . .

She was suddenly horrified with herself and plunged forward into the water. It felt ice-cold against her sun-warmed legs. Almost at once she was out of her depth and began to swim. She was a strong swimmer and enjoyed the exhilaration of diving through the breakers. She could see Blake Randall's shaggy grey head bobbing up and down, close beside hers.

She caught a glimpse of his brown, wet face, screwed up; heard him yell:

'Race you to that rock we sat on the other day, at low tide. Over there on the right. Can you manage it?'

'Think so!' she yelled back, and got a mouthful of salt water which left her gasping.

She over-estimated her own capacity. It was more than she could manage. When the rock was still fifty yards away from her, she felt her strength ebbing. The old pain was there, nagging at her back. Her heart was thumping. Her whole body felt the strain. She thought:

'I'm too old for this. It serves me right, trying to behave like a young girl!'

Dazzled by the sunlight, and with the pain clutching now at her heart, she let out a cry:

'Blake!'

He was swimming ahead of her and did not hear.

Clare had an instant's horror that she

might drown. She would never reach that rock. In a moment she would have to give up and go down, suffocating, swallowing water and *suffocating!* Horrible!

'Oh, Blake, help me!'

This time her voice reached him. He turned his head and saw her grey twisted face and short panic-stricken strokes. In a moment, he had turned and was swimming swiftly back to her on the tide. He reached her, put an arm under one of hers and shouted:

'Let yourself go! Stop swimming! Stop! I can manage you.'

She gave in gladly, gasping, eyes closed, feeling every vestige of strength slip away from her. And with it her consciousness.

When she opened her eyes again she was safely on that rock, feeling the blessed warmth and security of it under her. Blake Randall was chafing her hands, smoothing the wet strands of hair back from her face.

'My dear! My dear, are you all right?'

She gave a long sigh. The blood flowed back to her cheeks. Her heart began to beat more normally. She felt a little sick, but she had not swallowed enough water for it to matter much. The very fact that she had fainted and relaxed in his hold had made it easy for Blake to get her to the rocks. She put the back of her hand across her forehead to shade her eyes from the sun, and smiled up into his face. Why, he was quite a queer colour. She had given him a shock. He was panting, too.

'So sorry,' she whispered. 'Thought I could manage it.'

'I'm the one to be sorry. I ought never to have suggested it. God, what a turn you gave me! First of all I thought you'd got cramp.'

'No — just tired.'

'You lie here without moving for a moment. We can climb back over the rocks. You needn't swim again.'

She gave a shaky laugh.

'We've no shoes. We'll cut our feet on the mussels!'

'Better that than that you should drown, my child. You're not going into the water again.'

She laughed weakly and was horrified to find the tears gathering in her eyes. She was in a stupid, exhausted state. She whispered:

''The child', as you are pleased to call her, is a silly old fool who ought to give up swimming.'

That brought an unexpected answer from him. He looked at her as though he were furious. The yellow light flickered dangerously in his eyes.

'Will you stop calling yourself *'old'*. And will you please stop thinking you ought to give up anything, except behaving as though you were ninety, when you're still such a kid . . . '

Then he broke off, and with a sudden gesture, carried the small hand which he had been chafing to his lips. They were lips wet and salt from the sea, but the kiss was warm and deep. He added, huskily:

'Little Wicks, I thought you were

drowning just then. God! I'd never have forgiven myself.'

She was immeasurably touched that the incident should have affected him so. And the touch of his lips against her hand unnerved her to such an extent that she began to cry in earnest. The tears poured down her cheeks. She turned over on the rocks and hid her face on the crook of her arm. She had no idea why she was crying, neither had he. But it banished for him all remembrance of her husband — her family. He just gathered her straight into his arms.

'Darling!' he said. 'Darling!'

For a second, Clare Tardy clung to him quite helplessly and went on weeping. Her cheek pressed against the salt wetness of his. Her arms about his neck. Then he turned his head and kissed her mouth.

Had she abandoned herself utterly to that kiss, in her present state of mental and physical exhaustion, she might have said and done any foolish thing. But the very fact that Blake Randall's embrace was the most thrilling thing that had happened to her since that night when he had kissed her, twenty-one years ago, brought her to her senses. This would never, *never* do! It was madness! She ought to be thoroughly well ashamed of herself. And afterwards she would be. She knew it.

She drew away from him, pushing him almost violently from her. She sought refuge in humour. To be serious would be a disaster, so comic she must become. Wiping her eyes, she gave an hysterical laugh.

'Captain Randall! Captain *Randall!* And you know if Matron saw us she'd remove me from your ward and possibly from the hospital staff. Recollect yourself, sir! *If* you please.'

He made no answer. Neither did he smile. His whole body was trembling. But he saw what she was trying to do, and with a great effort, and for her sake alone, he controlled his desire to sweep her back into his arms. God! He thought that had been a divine and lovely moment against her lips. Old? She was young — as young as any girl, as unfledged, for all her great family. She had trembled like a girl in his arms. Her lips had been sweet and passionate under his. And he would give his soul to take her away and make her his love and his wife!

Clare struggled on to her feet.

'We must get back. Come along. Over the mussels we go, and thank God my husband's a doctor if we do cut our feet to pieces.'

Her husband. That brought Blake back to earth. Cracked his dreams over the head with a wallop. He had wanted to forget that this woman had a husband and that she was a faithful and devoted wife.

With bitterness in his heart, coupled with a great burning resentment against life, he picked his way over the sharp rocks and followed Clare back to the beach.

4

Downstairs in the lounge of the hotel, Miss Minter was enjoying herself.

'Do you know' — she greeted everybody who came in to tea — 'Mrs. Tardy was nearly drowned this afternoon!'

To which she received a variety of answers.

From a retired Colonel and his wife:

'Dangerous coast, this. Currents very treacherous. Not surprised someone's got into difficulties . . .'

From the mother of a large family:

'Women over forty shouldn't attempt to behave like young girls!'

From an Austrian boy, on his first visit to the English coast:

'*Ach so!* Poor lady! So sweet she is!'

And so on, until the whole hotel was buzzing with the news, and over tea it was passed from mouth to mouth until it was magnified out of all proportion, and finally bore little relation to the truth.

'Mr. Randall has saved Mrs. Tardy from a watery grave. She had gone down for the third time. Yes! Never nearer death! She is prostrate from the shock.'

When Dr. Tardy strolled into the lounge for tea, a dozen people whom he only knew by sight, approached him and asked for news. He seemed mildly surprised. His replies were disappointing.

'She is far from prostrate. Just resting. Nearly drowned? . . . Not at all. Lot of nonsense!'

He was not prepared to admit to anybody that his wife had been on the verge of a catastrophe. But personally, he had been shaken out of his equilibrium when he had first awakened from his slumbers on the beach to find Clare asking him to take her back to the hotel. She had looked a bad colour and was not at all herself.

However, she had only swum a little farther than she ought. He saw no reason why she should have taken it so badly. Usually she made light of any aches or pains. She had acceded without protest to his suggestion that she should lie down and have her tea sent upstairs.

Randall had apologized to him for making Clare swim so far, then disappeared.

When Christopher Fenlick's car came back from Newquay with the family, Miss Minter, who adored a drama, was ready on the porch to greet them with her exaggerated story.

'Your mother was very nearly drowned this afternoon!'

The four young people, who had thoroughly enjoyed their picnic, stood still with one accord and stared at Miss Minter. Jack, who had been on the verge of cracking a joke with Christopher, went quite white.

'Good God! How? Where?'

'She tried to swim out to Pilcher's

Point. Mr. Randall saved her.'

'Good heavens!' said Christopher.

'Oh, I *say!*' came from Mogs, her eyes goggling. 'Mr. Randall's saved Mummy's life. How *super!*'

Joan said nothing. But her eyes were so stricken that Christopher instinctively took her hand.

Then they all started to rush through the lounge, and up the stairs, making for Clare's bedroom

Clare, lying on her bed, the curtains drawn to keep out the sun because her head ached, was propped up on one elbow drinking a much-needed cup of tea when the whole family burst into her room.

Mogs was the first to reach her bedside.

'Mummy! Mummy! Say, you're not drowned!' was her dramatic cry. She flung herself on to the bed and put a hot, rather sandy face against Clare's.

Joan bent down.

'Mum, how *could* you! What happened?'

'You can't go doing things like that while we're away,' came from Jack, with a brightness he was far from feeling. The thought of his mother nearly drowning appalled him.

Christopher Fenlick hovered in the doorway anxiously, waiting for the others to come out and tell him that Mrs. Tardy was all right.

Clare found herself embracing them all, half-laughing, half-crying.

'But, darlings, I didn't nearly drown. What a lot of nonsense! Who said I did? Of course I'm all right. Absolutely. I just got a bit tired and Blake pulled me in. Who on earth gave you such an account?'

'Miss Minter said you nearly drowned,' said Mogs.

Clare hugged her.

'Idiot! I was nowhere near drowning.'

Jack patted his heart.

'Phew! I'll kill that woman for giving me such a turn.'

Joan's gaze sped to her mother's foot, on which she saw a large piece of plaster.

'How did you hurt your foot, Mum darling?'

'Cut it on a mussel, clambering back. Daddy did it up for me.'

'Where is Daddy?'

'He went down for tea. Didn't you see him? You'd better join him, darlings. You can see there's no need to worry about me.'

The three children looked down at their mother dubiously for a moment. Her eyelashes were wet. They had none of them ever seen tears in her eyes before. It made them embarrassed and unhappy. But in the dim light of the curtained room, there seemed nothing else much wrong with her. And she was smiling now, assuring them that there was nothing wrong.

They left her, promising to come up again after tea and tell her about their adventures in Newquay.

The door closed upon them.

Clare gave a great sigh and lay back on her pillow.

'What darlings they all are! What

darlings!' she thought.

The room was quiet again except for the rustle of the curtains as the sea-breeze blew them inward, then let them flap back again. For the second time that day she found herself crying. Her head, her whole body ached with a pain that was not purely physical. It was acute nervous strain. The shock of the moment when she had thought that she could swim no more had passed. But not so the shock of the discovery which she had made about herself and Blake. She had not been able to analyse herself or her emotions immediately after that intense moment in his arms. She had been too concerned with getting back to Guy, and trying to laugh and treat the whole episode as a joke. But when she entered the hotel, she had been not only supremely conscious of a critical state of mind, but of Blake, silent and tense, following them. Of his eyes upon her. Eyes that held a look which made her heart shake as though she were a young girl.

Lying here quietly, she saw what had happened to her. Something which she had not thought possible. At the age of forty-two, she was in love again. In love, after twenty-one years of calm, uneventful married life with Guy. Of course it was disgraceful! She had no right to allow herself to feel like this about Blake Randall. Guy was a faithful and devoted husband to her. And there were those children, those blessed, beloved children. How could she possibly be capable of such flagrant disloyalty toward them? How sweet they had been, rushing in here, horrified because they thought she had been near to drowning! They loved her. Independent they might be, living their own lives, but she was the main source of their lives. The being upon whom they relied and to whom they looked for most things. If she failed them or let them down, she would smash one of the greatest of their ideals. The ideal which most young people have about their mothers. If they thought for a single instant that she was

340

capable of embracing another man, they would be disgusted and ashamed of her. And rightly so.

That was the way in which Clare's conscience worked as she lay there, battling with herself. With her emotional self, which was not altogether Guy's or the children's. That side of her which was real woman, loving and needing to be loved.

She had known, with Blake Randall's lips against hers, that she was still young enough to feel passion in its fullest sense. That she could respond to him, perhaps all the more passionately, because she had so long been cheated and thwarted of such love.

Subconsciously, she had tackled this problem a dozen times in her life, but never actively. Never before had she actually faced such a crisis. There had not been another Blake. Nor another instant when her heart had beaten faster for another man. She had been too passive. She had accepted Guy and the unstimulating intimacy of their married life as normal and inevitable. She was deeply fond of him. That had seemed enough. But no! It hadn't been enough. Only, since Guy was her chosen man, she had abided by that choice. She had done away with that woman who had thrilled, out there on the rocks, in Blake's arms. Annihilated her, constituted herself simply and solely Guy's wife and the mother of his children. And that was how she must go on. She had travelled the path too long to take another course. Until she died, she must remain Guy's wife, and the mother of Jack, Joan and Mogs.

But her tears flowed desperately. She was weeping for that young Clare, that vital, restless Clare of long ago. The 'Little Wicks' who yearned for Blake Randall and all that might have been.

She wondered what unhappy fate had led her to choose this hotel, and so meet again the friend of her youth, know again the thrill of a kiss which she had long forgotten!

Wiping away her tears, she sought

valiantly to readjust the balance of her emotions and put herself to ridicule.

An old married woman. A matron, with sagging breasts, with hips that needed a good strong elastic belt to support them; a woman with greying hair and a constant pain across her back, and a tendency in winter to rheumatism.

That woman was all right to be the wife of Guy Tardy and the mother of children. But all wrong to be the breathless, trembling girl who had lain against Blake Randall's heart.

As for Blake, she could not begin to think what he found in her to like so much, nor why she had for him any physical appeal. It was all so queer, so ridiculous, and so horribly sad!

He was lonely, poor Blake. Of course, that's what it was. He had not *really* fallen in love with her. Only with the shadow of his Helen. And she might have helped him — might have made him happy again — if she had been free. (Was ever a woman less free — with all those family chains shackling her, hand and foot?)

The tears went on pouring down Clare's cheeks, bitter and scorching. Laugh at herself she could and must. But when she left Kymer Cove, she would never be quite the same Clare again. Never again know the absolute peace which Blake Randall's kiss and touch had so violently disturbed.

The door opened.

Guy Tardy entered the room and tiptoed to the bed.

'Feeling all right again, dear?'

She half-hid her face on her arm so that he should not see her crying.

'Miles better, thank you, Guy.'

'Foot not hurting?'

'Not a bit. It was just a scratch.'

He moved to one of the windows and parted the curtains sufficiently to let in a chink of sunshine.

'Feel you can sleep a bit, or shall I open these?'

'No,' she said in a muffled voice. 'My — my head aches. Don't draw them back.'

'It was a bit too much for you, that swim.'

'Yes. I was forgetting how old I was.'

'Well, your heart's all right. Your pulse was fine just now.'

She shut her eyes. Her lashes stiffened with drying tears.

'Aren't I lucky to have a distinguished physician for a husband!'

'Not so distinguished,' said Guy Tardy. 'And, by the way, that old fool downstairs has put a first-rate thriller round the hotel about your life being saved by Randall. The place is fairly buzzing with it.'

Clare gave a weak laugh.

'I thought Miss Minter was a half-wit when we first arrived.'

'The kids are eating an enormous tea. I told them not to come up and disturb you.'

'I'll be down for dinner,' she said.

'Well, I think I'll have an hour on the links. Jack says he'll play nine holes with me.'

Clare lifted her lashes and watched

Guy as he took his golf shoes out of the cupboard. He sat down, put them on and laced them up. Then he exchanged his khaki-linen coat for a Norfolk jacket. Like the rest of them, he had grown sunburned. It was not the deep tan which made Blake Randall's face so striking. It was that reddish colour which auburn-haired people are apt to turn. Unattractive. He looked an insignificant and unattractive man, with his semi-baldness and his mild blue eyes. Yet Clare was stricken with remorse because she had been disloyal to him in her heart. She had lived with him and cared for him too long to be resentful of him because he was her husband. He had always been good to her. And they had been through many things together through the long years of struggle. What right had another, more attractive man to enter her life and so enchant her that even for an instant she could turn her back upon Guy?

Suddenly her hand went out.

'Guy!'

A little surprised by the unexpected gesture, and with his golf-clubs over his shoulder, the doctor walked to the bedside and took his wife's outstretched fingers.

'Yes? What is it, dear?'

Her throat constricted. She could not speak, but smiled at him, shaking her head stupidly.

He did not understand. He did not try to. But he was vaguely aware that she was in some way mentally as well as bodily upset by her little adventure in the water. Poor old Clare! He'd never seen her so unstrung.

He bent and kissed her cheek.

'You're all right, aren't you, dear?' he said.

She kissed him back and whispered:

'Quite all right. Go along and enjoy your golf.'

After he had gone, she tried to sleep but could not. She kept thinking about Blake and wondering how she would feel when she faced him tonight.

Wondering, too, what his reactions were to this affair.

It was not long before she knew. Mogs was her next visitor. Mogs, having been asked not to disturb her mother, attempted to open the door very silently. It creaked, and she then called upon her mother's name in a whisper sibilant enough to wake any slumberer.

'Are you asleep, Mum?'

'No, darling. Come in,' said Clare.

Said Mogs:

'There's going to be a dance in the hotel tonight.'

'Is there?'

'Miss Minter's just told us. They're taking away the ping-pong table in that big room with the glass loggia. They're polishing the floor now. Isn't it a thrill?'

'Lovely, darling.'

'You will come down, won't you, Mum?'

'I don't know that I want to dance — '

'Oh, but you must. It'll be absolutely

spoiled if you don't come down and watch us, even if you don't dance.'

Clare squeezed the hot young hand which was thrust into hers. She could never resist a demonstration of affection from Mogs.

'I'll come, if you really want me to, and if my foot is better.'

'Of course! We all want you. And Joan's fearfully thrilled because Chris dances so well. Mum, Chris is *frightfully keen* on Joan. At Newquay they went off by themselves and Jack and I — '

'Tell me later, darling,' Clare interrupted gently.

She was not exactly in the mood to hear about the young lovers. No, at the moment, try as she would to be sane and sensible, she was filled with too much envy of these young things in love. She wanted to shut her eyes and ears to the thought of that kind of love.

Then Mogs said:

'Oh, Mum, why is Mr. Randall going away?'

Clare's heart seemed to miss a beat. She said:

'I didn't know he was.'

'Yes. Tomorrow. He came in from the village just now and told us he'd had a wire from his firm, and he's got to cut his holiday short and go up to London tomorrow.'

'What bad luck!'

'I think he's frightfully nice, Mum. Won't you miss — '

'Run along downstairs now, darling,' Clare broke in. 'You must forgive me if I don't want to talk. My head still aches.'

'Sorry!' said Mogs, planted a sticky kiss on her mother's forehead, and departed.

Clare lay still.

So he was running away! From her and from himself. Very wise. She knew perfectly well that that wire was concocted. He had told her that the firm would not want him for another ten days. Well — there it was! He would go away tomorrow and she would never see him again. Much better so. From every point of view.

This was Saturday. She would be here another week. Another week of the holiday without Blake who had made this last fortnight so heavenly.

With him would go all the excitement and the happiness and the youth which he had brought back to her. She must become again the Clare who would sit beside a dozing husband, or perform some service for one of the family, or gossip with the other matrons in the hotel. Well, that was the Clare-who-had-been before Blake Randall re-entered her life. She must be glad to become that Clare again. She must jeer remorselessly at the stranger — the new, foolish Clare who had found not only an old friend, but a lover.

She turned her face to the pillow.

'Blake!' she whispered. '*Blake*!'

5

'You see, Little Wicks, don't you?' said Blake Randall, 'that I had to clear out. I couldn't possibly stay after what happened to us today.'

'I do quite see,' said Clare.

They were standing alone out on the verandah. From inside the hotel came the strains of a dance-band broadcast over the radio. The hotel was gay tonight. Everybody was in the ping-pong room, where the dancing was in full swing.

Guy was there, watching the children. Joan and Chris had danced every number together so far. Mogs had found a boy of her own age, shy, hot and sticky, who pranced about with her, treading on her toes at every step. Nevertheless, she seemed to find it satisfactory. Clare had danced twice. Once with her son. And once with

Blake Randall. She had not meant to do so. But when Blake had come up to her and reminded her that he had always wanted to dance with her in hospital and hadn't been able to, and she had realized that this would probably be the first and last time she ever *would* dance with him, she had consented.

She had thought herself strong. She had girded herself with armour before she had come down to dinner and faced at the table, not only the merry young party, but Blake. She had been the cheeriest of them all, declaring that she was none the worse for her 'drowning'. As the heroine of the evening, she had been congratulated by the entire hotel on her 'escape'. And, a nice touch from Miss Minter, she had been presented with a bunch of pink roses. Joan had made her pin one of them on her black chiffon dress. The dinner-party had been festive indeed. Guy, departing from his usual habit of drinking a whisky and soda, had ordered two bottles of hock. They had all toasted her, and then Blake for saving her life. And they had all laughed, knowing that it was exaggerated and absurd but enjoying it.

But there was a chink in her armour. Blake's arm about her and the look in his eyes while they danced had found a way through it to the woman inside. They had only taken a few turns round the room, then she had protested that she could dance no more. So he had brought her out here into the darkness. Here, where it was dark except for the stars. They could see the winking light of a ship on the horizon but not the sea. They could hear the rhythmic beat of the waves against the rocks below them and the booming from the distant caves.

A tremendous sadness enveloped Clare as she stood there beside this man whom she might have loved so well. He felt it in her, and also within himself.

'I've got to clear out,' he repeated.

'It's just as well,' she said.

'Walk with me a little way in the garden.'

'I must get back to the family — ' she began.

'They will have you for the rest of your life,' he broke in with sudden passion, 'and I won't.'

Her head drooped. She went with him, shivering slightly as the cool sea-breeze struck through the black chiffon of the little cape belonging to her dress. He could just discern the pale and lovely contour of her face. He knew every line, every shadow of it. He had hardly been able to stop looking at her during dinner tonight. He was very much in love with this woman, and it was a love which was not conscious of any strangeness or absurdity because of her family. That tall boy. That girl who was, herself, on the verge of a love-affair. That jolly, healthy schoolgirl, Mogs.

He loved their mother in spite of the fact that she was over forty. He felt that he would have loved her had she been fifty. To him she would always be 'Little Wicks' — the one woman in the world who might have taken Helen's place.

Bitterly he resented all the obstacles which were in the way of his taking what he wanted. Yet he resigned himself to them without even attempting to overcome one of them.

'You know, don't you, my dear,' he said, 'that I love you and that if you had been free I would have asked you to marry me?'

'Yes.'

'Would you have done so?'

'Yes.'

He pressed her arm close to his side.

'You're so very lovely. So very dear to me.'

'I oughtn't to let you say so. I oughtn't to be here listening to you. I oughtn't even to tell you what I feel!' she cried.

'Never mind the 'ought nots'. Let's just be honest with each other for a few moments. You needn't think yourself disloyal. I've never in my life met a woman more loyal. If all wives were like you, Little Wicks, the divorce courts would have to close down.'

'I don't agree. I feel that I've been very disloyal to Guy tonight.'

'By just saying that you would have married me if you could?'

'Yes.'

'Well, I'm afraid I can't regret that. At least I've got a memory to take away with me when I go to Canada. The memory that you might have said 'yes'.'

She gave a long sigh.

'I shall miss you, Blake.'

'I shall miss you, too, hellishly. It's been pretty marvellous, being with you. You're so different from any other woman. And there is just something between us — well — you know, don't you?'

'I know.'

'I daren't go on seeing you, darling.'

The endearment wrung her heart.

'I understand. And it's much better for me, too. I shall have to settle down to the old life and forget about you,

Blake. No, but I won't forget about you. I'll have my memories, too.'

He stopped and took both her hands, making her face him.

'Little Wicks, I can't bear to think you're going to be unhappy.'

'I won't be. I promise. You know Guy's awfully good to me. And the children are adorable.'

'That's why I haven't even begun to ask you to cut away and come with me.'

'You've been grand.'

'And this is where I say goodbye. I'm leaving Kymer by the first train. And I shall leave England as soon as my company can manage to send me abroad.'

'So for the second time you'll fade out of my life. Only, this time, I shall never see you again.'

'Perhaps in another twenty-one years?'

She gave a faint laugh.

'I shall be sixty-three and without doubt a grand-mother.'

'Don't!' he said roughly.

'Well, it's true. And you may be

married to somebody else. Oh, I want you to be! I don't want you to be lonely, Blake.'

'I won't marry now. There was never anybody for me but Helen, until I met you, and now — well, I'd rather go on being alone.'

There came a faint sound from the hotel. A familiar sound to Clare.

'Mum-my! Mum-my!'

'That's Mogs,' she said. 'And that's the call I've got to answer for the rest of my life, my dear.'

'Oh, my darling!' he said.

And swiftly he pulled her into his arms and kissed her on the mouth as he had kissed her this afternoon. Not once, but twice. Long and desperate kisses. Kisses for them both to remember in the days ahead.

Then she said:

'Goodbye, darling, darling Blake.'

She broke away from him. Smoothing her hair with one hand and holding her chiffon skirt with the other, she ran back to the hotel. She arrived on the verandah, out of breath and panting. Mogs was there, calling dismally, with a large rent in her blue taffeta dress.

'Oh, Mum — Frankie put his foot through my skirt. What *am* I to do? It's the only party dress I've brought with me and I *do* so want to go on dancing.'

Clare, trying to gather herself together, saw that Mogs' face was screwed up as though she were going to cry. She banished the memory of the man whom she had left in the garden. She said:

'Come along upstairs and we'll find a needle and thread quickly and pull it together somehow.'

'Joan said you couldn't, but I *knew* you would,' said Mogs with relief and with the confidence of one who felt that here, always, whatever happened, her faith would not be placed in vain.

6

That next morning was one on which Clare would have chosen to sleep; to be unconscious of the moment in which Blake Randall left the Headland Hotel and boarded the Cornish Express which would take him out of her life.

But it was also the morning on which Dr. Tardy and his son chose to go bass-fishing before breakfast.

They arranged it after the dance, and told Clare their plans.

It wasn't too hot, before breakfast, and the tide would be coming in. They would have a couple of hours' fishing from half-past six, then join the family for breakfast.

That put a finish to Clare's hopes of sleeping. She had had a bad night anyhow. Long before Guy was awake, her eyes opened only to find that dawn was just breaking, filling the bedroom with grey pearly light, bringing her back with a sense of shock to the realization of all that had happened yesterday.

There can be nothing sharper than the pain of an early morning awakening when something is wrong. That swift return to unhappy consciousness and the dread of facing a new day with misery in one's heart.

It was many years since Clare Tardy had experienced such a moment; and perhaps never before such a dark and hopeless one. For a while she lay staring at the window before her, watching the day grow lighter, listening to the plaintive screaming of the gulls, and realizing how suddenly and completely her life had gone awry.

This holiday had brought her face to face with the knowledge that she was still young enough to love and be loved. But it was not to be. Last night, she and Blake had said goodbye. Those thrilling raptures of returning youth, that feverish intensity of emotion, must be stamped upon ruthlessly and allowed to die as swiftly as they had come to birth.

Yet when she thought about Blake, the ache within her grew almost past endurance.

At length she sat up in bed, reached for a cigarette, lit it and sat there smoking in the half-darkened room, feeling utterly wretched.

Beside her lay Guy, peacefully asleep. She envied him that blessed unconsciousness and the peace in his mind and heart. Dear solid, placid Guy! As innocent of turbulent emotions and agonies as Mogs herself. Lucky Guy, to feel himself utterly fulfilled, as she knew that he did. Content with his emotional life, such as it was, and with his work. The rare moments when he held her, his wife, in his arms were sufficient for him. Romance had touched him once, lightly, and left him just the quiet concrete affections which he felt for her and for his children.

Yet, did she envy him? Could she not be glad that life had given her a moment with Blake? Was she not richer for the experience? Richer, spiritually, though physically still unassuaged.

She wondered what Guy would say to her if she told him about Blake. He would not understand. They had been so long married and together, he would not believe it possible that she could fly, even for an instant, to another man's arms. He would be hurt and bewildered. He had great kindliness. He might be sorry for her. But he would, of course, be bitterly disappointed. Ashamed that the mother of his children should so conduct herself. To tell him could bring them no nearer. It might send them farther apart. So not for her the luxury of confession about Blake Randall to Guy or any human being on earth. In the eyes of her children she must remain the pattern of virtuous and respectable womanhood. *Virtuous!* Clare stabbed the end of her cigarette in the ash-tray and hid her head in her hands. A most unvirtuous longing to recapture last night's ecstasy seized her. For a while she strove with herself, turning the things over and over in her mind. She had been a good wife to Guy. A good mother to the children. She would never fail them. She would try not to fail them in the future. But she wanted so desperately to feel Blake Randall's kiss upon her mouth once more.

She was up in an hour's time, waving goodbye to Guy and Jack who, with their fishing-rods and tackle, disappeared over the cliff-edge down the zigzag path to the beach.

Guy had been in very good humour while he dressed. More talkative than usual. He was really no older in spirit than Jack at times, she thought. Always at his best on a holiday. And Jack — the mother's heart yearned over her son — her fine handsome Jack. He had looked the picture of health, this morning. Eager for his fishing, his favourite sport. And for some reason — just a coincidence — he had chosen to be especially nice to her when she had walked through the hotel gardens with him to the edge of the cliff. He liked her, he said, in those grey flannel trousers which she was wearing with a fisherman's jersey and gay handkerchief scarf.

'You really are absurd, Mum. You look so young, and rather like me, this morning, with your hair brushed back that way.'

Her arm tucked through his, she had rubbed her cheek affectionately against his shoulder and said:

'I'm glad you don't think I'm an old fogey yet.'

'Fogey be blowed!' was his reply. 'You're a damned good-looking girl, Mum. My only girlfriend, if it comes to that.'

She couldn't answer him, but her eyelids stung with tears when she turned away from him. What would this son of hers think if he knew what lay in her heart?

She whispered to herself:

'I won't let you down, Jack. I won't. But I must see him once more . . . just once!'

And at seven o'clock she saw him.

Blake Randall came down to an early breakfast. He was catching the eight o'clock express to Paddington. He strolled out of the hotel and found Clare sitting on the steps, knees hunched up, chin supported on her hands. A forlorn little figure. The figure of the 'Little Wicks' of twenty-one years ago, rather than the woman of forty-two who had borne and reared a family.

Something caught him by the throat at the sight of her. He had not expected to find her down at this hour. He did not know whether to be glad or sorry, but he had had a hellish night. The freshness and beauty of the early summer morning meant nothing. It might have been raining and blowing a sou'wester gale for all he cared. He was leaving Kymer Cove in an hour's time, and that meant leaving this beloved woman who could never belong to him.

She turned her head and saw him. An unfamiliar Blake, with scrupulously groomed hair and wearing a dark lounge-suit which at once suggested 'London'.

Her gaze held his for a second. Then he sat down beside her.

'Well, my dear,' he said.

'Well, Blake.'

'I didn't expect to see you.'

'No. I had to get up. Guy and Jack have gone fishing.'

They both looked toward the misty blue of the sea. There was a faint haze around the Gull Rock. A little wind beat the blue-green water and sent sudden spurts of white spray into the air. The gulls were wheeling and circling in their hundreds, diving for their food. The sun caught their wet wings and made their plumage look iridescent, sparkling.

Said Blake:

'It'll be hot today.'

'Yes.'

'Did the children enjoy the dance?'

'Immensely. Mogs has a new 'crush'. The fat little boy called Frankie who put his foot through her dress.'

They both laughed, but the laughter was strained. Then Blake said:

'She's a grand kid. I like all your children. I thought at first Joan was going to be a bit difficult. These young girls of today are so dictatorial, and I didn't much like the way she laid down the law to you, but — '

'Oh, she doesn't mean it,' broke in Clare. 'And she's really been much more friendly and easier since she came here.'

'Yes, I think she's improved a lot in the short space of time I've known her. As for your son — well, I envy you that boy. He's great, and he'll go a long way. I hope they all like me. I wanted them to.'

'They do — all of them, Blake.'

Silence a moment. Neither of them mentioned Guy. Neither of them wanted to. Then Blake Randall looked at his wrist-watch.

'I'd better go in and eat my breakfast. Will you come in and talk to me? Nobody else is down.'

She nodded. He stood up and gave her his hand. She took it and he pulled her to her feet. She looked up into those queer, sad, tawny eyes of his. She shook her head mutely as though overcome by her own feelings.

'Darling,' he said gently.

Holding her hand tightly, he walked with her into the dining-room.

A yawning waiter, looking dilapidated and pallid in his evening clothes, resenting this early breakfast, was putting Mr. Randall's meal on the table which he had for the last fortnight shared with the Tardys.

Clare took a chair opposite Blake. She watched him tackle sausages and bacon. She poured out his coffee, smiling a little to herself. She couldn't have eaten a thing. But he could and did make a hearty breakfast, which seemed to her so like a man. As a sex, men could manage to eat in the most trying circumstances.

But in spite of the hearty meal, Blake Randall was an unhappy man and she knew that and was as sorry for him as for herself.

'I shall like to remember this in the days to come,' he said. 'You, sitting there pouring out my coffee, looking an absolute kid in those trousers.'

She smiled.

'Jack called me his 'girlfriend' this morning.'

'Well, I won't be jealous of that.'

'You needn't be jealous of anything, Blake.'

He leaned back in his chair and lit a cigarette.

'But I am, my dear. Jealous of every moment the family will spend with you for the rest of your life.'

She leaned her elbows on the table and interlaced her fingers. There was utter restlessness within her.

'I don't know how I'm going to settle down again.'

'You will, because you're brave, my dear. You always had courage. Do you remember that night at Camberley when they thought there was going to be an air raid? Little Wicks, cool as a cucumber, rounding us all up and telling us not to get the wind-up if we heard a bomb drop. Helping Sister drill the orderlies as to who was to be carried out first, and where.'

'I remember.'

'We'll always have those days to look back on, Little Wicks.'

'And do you remember, Blake, that fat little officer — I can't remember his name, we called him Tubby — who used to take the hard-boiled eggs which were left for the night nurses' supper? He was so greedy! And when we found half a dozen of the eggs under his mattress?'

'Lord, yes! And that Major bloke with the becoming sun-tan who thought himself such a lad with the nurses. Do you remember we found a bottle of sun-bronze in his cupboard and we all got hold of him and covered him in it, not only his face!'

A sparkle came into Clare's eyes and a little colour in the face which had been so much paler than usual this morning.

'*Wasn't* that fun?'

They smiled into each other's eyes. Then the smile died and the happy recollections faded until there was nothing left between them but the sharp pain of the present.

Blake said abruptly:

'I've got five minutes before the car comes to take me to the station. I'll tell the porter to get my luggage down. Let's go out.'

She went with him into the garden. The sun was yet higher. The radiance of a perfect August morning shimmered against their faces as they came out of the hotel.

By mutual consent, they found their way to that corner of the garden in which they had stood last night. A great clump of tamarisk hid them from the hotel. And here, once again, Clare was drawn into her lover's arms.

'I can't bear to leave you,' he said.

'But I've got to, my dear. I couldn't stay, could I?'

She clung to him for a moment, thankful for the warmth and strength of his arms about her. She felt so very tired.

'No, you must go,' she said. 'But the days are going to be very long without you, Blake.'

'I'll never forget you, Little Wicks. That's how I'll think of you, as 'Little Wicks', and not — '

'Not the old lady with grey hairs,' she put in, and muffled a laugh against his shoulder.

'I adore her, too. Oh, darling, I shall have to go. I can hear the car.'

Fear smote Clare Tardy's heart. She was frightened of letting him go. For when he went, it seemed that he would take all the love and laughter out of her life.

For a long moment they kissed. Then she drew away from him and turned her back so that he should not see the tears that were raining down her cheeks.

'Goodbye — darling — Blake.'

'Try to be happy, Little Wicks,' he said. And with the greatest effort left her alone, standing with her face hidden in her hands.

She heard the hum of the car as it drove away, and wondered for an instant's agony how she could go on.

But she knew that she must go on. And she knew that if she asked to keep Blake, it would be demanding too much of life altogether. She had her husband and her children, and so much more than nine women out of ten. She had no right to complain because the ultimate joys and ecstasies were not for her.

Wiping the tears from her eyes, she stood a while longer where he had left her, letting the warm sunlight drench her from head to foot.

It was there that Joan found her. Joan, who had risen earlier than usual, because she had a date for an early swim with Christopher.

The mother saw her coming along

with her easy, youthful stride. A gay, charming Joan in a white swim-suit and blue cape, swinging her cap and towel in her hand. A Joan who hailed her cheerfully.

'Morning, Mum! Chris and I are going down to bathe. Did Jack and Pop go after their bass?'

'Yes, darling.'

'I say, it's rotten that Mr. Randall had to go off this morning. I've just said goodbye to him. He's been such fun. We shall miss him, shan't we?'

Clare nodded, not trusting herself to speak.

And suddenly, Joan Tardy noticed her mother's face. It looked pinched and her eyes were heavy. Almost as though she had been crying. But *surely* not!

A dozen conjectures flashed into Joan's mind. A rather jumbled young mind, not very clear about things, but with a certain shrewd perception and understanding. Of *course!* Mr. Randall had been one of Mummy's 'flames' during the war. She must have had a grand time with him these last two weeks. He was so amusing. A much better sort of companion than Daddy, bless his old heart. And hadn't Anthony Downe once pointed out that life need not finish for a woman because she was forty? Why, surely, Mummy and Mr. Randall . . . ?

Joan cut her reflections short. It was none of her business, and probably she was all wrong. But if she were right, it was pretty rotten for poor old Mum! She always did so much for them. After all, she got little out of it, herself, so far as Joan could see.

Joan was by nature a tactful and thinking person. And this morning she rose to an occasion. Suddenly, she went to her mother, put an arm about her and kissed her cheek.

'We've had such a gorgeous holiday, darling. And we owe it all to you. And I, particularly, want you to know how much I appreciate everything you do.'

Clare stood speechless. Such rare demonstration of affection from her elder daughter bowled her over. But she had never been more in need of that appreciation nor of all that was underlying it. To know that she meant much to her family — to be loved by them — would help and comfort her, make it so much easier for her to resign herself to the loss of that other love.

She returned Joan's kiss. In silence, mother and daughter walked back to the hotel, their arms around each other.

They passed by the yew, clipped to the shape of a fox, on the front lawn. Joan did not even notice it. For nowadays, it could only revive the most cold and disdainful memories of Anthony Downe. Christopher Fenlick had so secure and warm a place in her mind and heart, there was room for no other man and no other memory.

BOOK SEVEN

Downstairs, in the basement of Dr. Tardy's house, Lucy lectured the baker's boy.

'Coming at four when you were asked to deliver the loaves directly after lunch! And My People coming back from their holiday, too. What d'you think would have happened if they'd got here hungry for tea and no bread?'

The boy, a smart young man with oily black hair and a wicked eye, grinned at Lucy and her wrath.

'Well, they ain't here, and they ain't going hungry and you've got your loaves. What's the worry?'

Lucy took the bread and handed it majestically to Gerda who stood behind her, smiling in her dazzling fashion at the handsome baker's boy.

'Get on with cutting that bread and butter,' said Lucy.

There came the sound of a horn. A shrill blare familiar enough to Lucy. She ran to the window and looked through the iron bars, rolling down her sleeves.

'It's them, Gerda. It's them! Here! Where's me cuffs? Leave the bread and butter now. Come up and help with the luggage.'

There was a distinct moisture in the pale, baleful eyes of Lucy as she mounted her dark little staircase and went to meet her people. She had missed them. The holiday with her mother had been dull. She had been glad to get back to London and clean up the house and realize that life, as she had spent it for the last twenty years, was beginning again.

Even in her excitement, she had time to pause in the hall and straighten the rug. She cast a suspicious glance at the umbrella stand. Was the doctor's umbrella there? And the Missus' blue silk with the ivory handle? And Master Jack's Malacca cane? She was sure that one day, somebody would come to the front door and 'lift' one of the precious articles out of that stand.

Having satisfied herself that everything was in its place, she threw open the front door.

There stood 'The Tortoise', all doors open, and five people tumbling out. A wild jumble of suitcases, hold-alls, rackets, golf-clubs, packages. Always the packages full of the little things which had been forgotten until the trunks were locked. Articles that could not be forced into suitcases strained already to their uttermost limit. Why was it, thought Lucy, that the family always came back from this holiday with so much more than they took? And those sodden parcels of wet bathing-suits and wraps which had been used an hour or two before saying goodbye to the sea! Ugh!

Mogs, always the first anywhere, flung herself at Lucy.

'Hallo! We've had a *super* time. Look how brown I've got! And I can swim farther than anybody now, except Mummy, and she nearly got drowned . . . '

'Shut up, Mogs. We're fed up with that story,' cut in Jack. He was feeling cross and in need of a long drink, having driven for the last fifty miles.

Mogs thrust a tin of cream into Lucy's hand and danced into the house, where Gerda received her with little soft German exclamations:

'*Ach! Mein liebes Kind! Wie geht's?*'

Jack patted Lucy's arm.

'Hallo, Beautiful! For the love of Mike, fetch me a glass of beer.'

Lucy, beaming at her handsome, cherished Master Jack, coyly assumed the disapproval which she so often felt in truth.

'Beer, indeed! With your tea all waiting.'

She'd never seen the family look so fine. Particularly Miss Joan, who seemed radiant and had an unusually hearty greeting for her, and a whisper which set her all agog.

'I've got some *news* for you, Lucy.'

Then the doctor. He was always the same. Ready with a kind word.

'How's Lucy? Yes, thank you, we had a very good Holiday.'

And now the Mistress. Ah! Here was one who didn't look so well. Lucy's shrewd eye detected immediately signs of fatigue and depression in Clare. She walked up the steps to the front door, carrying her small leather case and a coat over her arm. She was brown all right, but looked properly tired out.

Lucy took the case from her.

'How are you, m'm? What you want is a nice cup of tea, I'll be bound.'

'Thank you, Lucy,' said Clare, as she entered the hall, and added: 'How lovely and clean everything's looking.'

Jack dropped a heap of things in the hall and returned to the car where his father was unstrapping the trunks. Gerda was climbing the stairs to the bedrooms, suitcases in either hand, followed by Mogs, who chattered wildly of her adventures.

Clare let Lucy take her hat and the

little linen jacket which she was wearing. She smoothed back her hair wearily.

'I could do with that cup of tea.'

'You shall have it now, m'm. And I've got dinner all ordered. I thought a nice joint would be the thing as you was all going to be in, and a nice greengage tart.'

Clare smiled. That brought her back home, indeed!

'It sounds all right to me, Lucy. We brought back some Cornish cream. We can have that with the tart.'

She walked into the dining-room where tea had been laid. Lucy's idea of a welcome was evident in the iced cake with cherries on it and the little scones made from sour milk which all the children liked.

With the most curious feeling that the whole of the last three weeks had been unreal, Clare stood at the window and watched her husband and son deal with the luggage. She drew a case from her bag, took out a cigarette and lit it.

While she smoked, here in this familiar room, waiting for Lucy's 'nice cup of tea', she looked back on the holiday in a kind of daze. A daze that had not really left her since that morning when Blake Randall had said goodbye. Dear, *dear* Blake who had gone away carrying with him such a big, important piece of her heart. A piece which she felt that even the family would not begrudge her having given him. There were so many important bits left behind for them.

The last week of the holiday at Kymer had been difficult for Clare. Horribly difficult to readjust herself, and get back her sense of proportion and her sense of humour. The days without Blake had seemed to her frankly blank and dead. But she had had to get over that feeling and make sure that not one of the others so much as guessed how much she missed her friend. And if she was a little quiet and preoccupied, she hoped they put it down to physical reasons. She could always blame it on the shock of that 'drowning'.

The development of a love-affair between Joan and Chris Fenlick had helped her. At first she had thought she could not bear to see Joan's budding raptures. But that was crass selfishness which she had conquered. She had never been a dog-in-the-manger, and after all, it was Joan's turn. Joan had a right to happiness and she, Clare, had no right to the kind of happiness which Blake had brought.

It was the day before they left Kymer Cove that Chris and Joan had come back from a long walk and told her that they wanted to become engaged. Dear Joan! And after all the things she used to say about Chris! It was curious that they should have come together in the end. It delighted Clare. She had never liked any of Jack's Oxford friends more than the young artist. Guy felt that way about him, too.

Of course, it would have to be a long engagement. Chris wouldn't be able to support a wife for a couple of years. But Joan wasn't nineteen yet, so there was plenty of time. Meanwhile, it gave Clare a warm, contented feeling about her daughter. She felt that she need never again go through that secret, gnawing anxiety which she had felt about her during the Anthony Downe period.

Joan had been particularly sweet and unselfish to her during that last week at Kymer, as though her instinct had told her that all was not well with her mother and it had been her way of expressing her sympathy. Nothing had been said between them, but it had forged yet another link in the chain which bound Clare to this grown-up daughter of hers.

Things were all right with Jack, too. Work was his main objective, he said, and it seemed a good one. And she no longer had to worry about the unknown girl. That doubt had been settled the night before they went on holiday. Gerda had come to her with a photograph which was torn in half, saying that she had found it in Mr. Jack's basket, and wondered whether it ought to be thrown away or pasted together.

For which piece of stupidity, Clare was grateful to Gerda. She knew that torn photograph of the girl in Oxford was meant for the flames, and she appreciated the significance.

While she stood there smoking, Gerda came in with a bundle of letters on a salver and handed them to her.

Clare took them and sorted the accumulation of bills, receipts and circulars which had been thrust through the door during the last three weeks. Nothing had been sent on to Kymer.

There was one letter from her aunt in Harrogate. An invitation to dinner from a doctor's wife in Earls Court. And suddenly, there emerged from the pile of halfpenny envelopes and sales-catalogues, a square white envelope, with a crest on the flap, which brought the colour hotly to her cheeks.

She opened the envelope with fingers

that shook a little.

This was from Blake Randall. The first he had ever sent her. The last he would ever write. He had written it on board twenty-four hours ago, and it had been posted before the liner sailed.

'*Dear Little Wicks,*
    '*In a few hours I sail for Canada. I take with me the memory of a perfect holiday.*
    '*Goodbye and God bless you.*
                                '*Blake.*'

She read it twice. Then, with tears stinging her eyelids, screwed it up into a little ball, walked away from the window and swallowed hard, trying to master herself.

It was nice of Blake to have written. She was glad he had thought of her just before he sailed. But it was almost unbearable to know how completely he had gone from her now.

Lucy came into the room with the large, Georgian silver teapot and hot-water-jug which they only used when they were all in for tea. Mogs followed, waving a letter in the air.

'I've passed, Mummy! I've passed!'

'What, darling?'

'My Intermediate. And it was *frightfully* hard. Even Miss Walters said so.'

'How pleased Miss Walters will be,' said Clare.

Mogs wrinkled a sunburned, peeling nose.

'Pooh! I don't care about her. I've just taken her photograph down from my wall and put up a snap of Frankie. Frankie is simply sweet. Can we ask him to stay? And Mum — isn't it super? — Chris and Joan say I can be a bridesmaid when they get married.'

Clare embraced her.

'Congratulations on the music, pet. Go and tell Daddy. He'll be pleased.'

Guy and Jack walked into the dining-room. They were both examining their letters which had been thrust into their hands by the smiling Gerda. Guy looked across at his wife who had seated herself at the table and begun to pour out tea.

'I see there's a message on my pad, dear. Todd wants me to go round to his home for a consultation as soon as I'm back. I left him in charge of an important patient, and she's been difficult. He thinks I ought to see her at once. I won't stop for tea.'

'Just a cup?' said Clare.

'Well, just a cup, dear. But I've got to change my clothes and get along as soon as I can.'

Jack flung himself into a chair beside his mother.

'Poor old Pop! Nose back to the grindstone.'

'Well, well!' said Guy, 'we had a very good holiday, and I don't mind getting back to work. I like it.'

'I shan't mind getting back either, really,' said Jack.

And he began to spread a scone with jam and cream, feeling happier than he had felt for weeks. Gosh! It was a relief to get that letter from old Withers who said that the Deering sisters had suddenly given up the dancing school and left Oxford. The one thing that had been weighing on Jack's mind was the fear that he might run into Amanda next term. The place would seem a darn sight nicer without her. He wondered whether she had gone because of what he had found out? Well, he didn't care what had happened. He was just glad he would never see her again.

Joan joined the family.

'Tea without milk or sugar for me, Mum. I've put on too much weight at Kymer and I'm going to get slim again.'

Jack grinned at her.

'Is this to please the artist's eye?'

Joan's colour rose.

'Maybe it is. Chris hates fat girls.'

'What it is to be in lu-uv!' said Jack, rolling his eyes.

'Shut up!' she said, with a swift kick under the table.

Mogs seized a scone.

'Ooh, I'm hungry. I wish we were back at Kymer Cove. Oh, lawks! Mum, I believe I left my snap-album in the top drawer of my dressing-table.'

'I told you to look through the drawers,' said Joan.

Clare sat back in her chair and drank down her tea.

'We've never had a holiday yet that something hasn't been left behind.'

'You young people are very careless,' admonished Dr. Tardy, and speedily left the room to change into more professional garb.

'Well, I can write to Miss Minter,' said Mogs cheerfully.

'God bless Miss Minter,' said Jack, and gulped his tea with a great sucking sound which drew a shudder from Joan.

'Pig!'

'I wonder if we shall ever have such a lovely holiday again?' sighed Mogs.

'Never,' said Joan fervently, and thought how marvellous tomorrow would be. Christopher was taking her out to choose her engagement ring.

'Never,' said Clare softly, sitting back in her chair. She smiled, shut her eyes, and saw a great white liner putting out to sea.

THE END

We do hope that you have enjoyed reading this large print book.

Did you know that all of our titles are available for purchase?

We publish a wide range of high quality large print books including:
Romances, Mysteries, Classics
General Fiction
Non Fiction and Westerns

Special interest titles available in large print are:
The Little Oxford Dictionary
Music Book, Song Book
Hymn Book, Service Book

Also available from us courtesy of Oxford University Press:
Young Readers' Dictionary
(large print edition)
Young Readers' Thesaurus
(large print edition)

For further information or a free brochure, please contact us at:
Ulverscroft Large Print Books Ltd.,
The Green, Bradgate Road, Anstey,
Leicester, LE7 7FU, England.
Tel: (00 44) 0116 236 4325
Fax: (00 44) 0116 234 0205

Other titles in the
Linford Romance Library:

SECOND TIME AROUND

Margaret Mounsdon

Widowed single parent Elise Trent thought no one could replace her husband Peter, until she met policeman Mark Hampson. She is forced to seriously re-think her life when her mother-in-law Joan accepts a proposal of marriage from long time companion Seth Baxter, and her student daughter Angie and Mark's son Kyle get involved with an action group. Then Elise and Mark are further thrown together by a spate of country house burglaries . . .